ALSO BY MALLORY ORTBERG

Texts from Jane Eyre

The

Merry

Spinster

The Merry Spinster

Tales of
Everyday Horror

Mallory Ortberg

A HOLT PAPERBACK

HENRY HOLT AND COMPANY

NEW YORK

Holt Paperbacks
Henry Holt and Company
Publishers since 1866
175 Fifth Avenue
New York, New York 10010
www.henryholt.com

Library of Congress Cataloging-in-Publication Data is available.

ISBN: 9781250113429

Our books may be purchased in bulk for promotional, educational, or business
use. Please contact your local bookseller or the Macmillan Corporate and
Premium Sales Department at (800) 221-7945, extension 5442, or by e-mail at
MacmillanSpecialMarkets@macmillan.com.

First Edition 2018

Designed by Meryl Sussman Levavi

Printed in the United States of America

1 3 5 7 9 10 8 6 4 2

For Nicole Cliffe

t'hy'la

With that Christian brake out with a loud voice: Oh, I see him again! and he tells me, "When thou passest through the waters, I will be with thee, and through the rivers, they shall not overflow thee."

Then they both took courage, and the enemy was after that as still as a stone, until they were gone over. Christian therefore presently found ground to stand upon; and so it followed that the rest of the river was but shallow. Thus they got over.

—JOHN BUNYAN, *The Pilgrim's Progress*

Contents

The

Merry

Spinster

ONE

The Daughter Cells

DAUGHTERS ARE AS GOOD A THING AS ANY TO populate a kingdom with—if you've got them on hand. They don't cost much more than their own upkeep, which you're on the hook for regardless, so it's not a bad strategy to put them to use as quickly as possible. There are, you may know, kingdoms underneath the sea as well as above it, with all manners of governance, as it happens. Kings have daughters there too, in the manner of kings everywhere, and fathers there must find something to do with daughters, just as we do on land. There once was a king who owned a great deal of what lay under the surface of the sea, and he happened to fill it with his daughters. Another man might have filled it with something else—potato farmers or pop-eyed scholars or merchant marines—but this one filled it with daughters, so there's no use arguing about it now.

Each of this man's daughters had a little plot of ground in the central gardens of the underwater city, which she could develop as she liked. Each daughter had use of the land but did not own it. (I haven't time to explain to you the way personal property is thought about in states where all borders are by definition liquid. There are other books about that sort of thing.) You might call the daughters princesses. I wouldn't, but if it's easier for you, then you might. You might call them something else, too—there are words for such things that live under the sea and haven't legs. You certainly wouldn't think to call them *girls*, if you happened to see them.

At any rate, these girls didn't own their patches of land, but they had the use of them, which made for good practice. They might ornament their allotted land with flowers, they might grow crops, or they might stuff it with old sea glass and bits of shipwrecked kettles, as they saw fit. The only way to teach the value of something is to give someone the chance to waste it—or at least that was how the thinking went under that particular administration. And most of the daughters grew up with a reasonably discerning sense of what was worth something and what wasn't, so that's one point in that philosophy's favor. Most of them didn't farm sea glass either.

The youngest of the daughters planted nothing at all in her garden, and no one thought any less of her for it. If a single polyp so much as presented its head above the ground there, she'd twist it out and fling it over the wall before it could so much as think of partitioning itself. She had no particular genius for growing things, and saw no reason to force a skill when there were so many others to cultivate.

You might well ask—and some did—why bother to go to all the trouble of patrolling for kelp and rhizomes and bits of eelgrass if you weren't going to grow anything in their place. "The point isn't that I'm growing anything else there, at least not at present," she always said. "There's the whole rest of the sea available to go be a polyp or a rhizome or a bit of eelgrass in; they just can't do it *here*. I can go look at a flower anywhere without having to put in a lot of effort to grow a poorer version of my own," which everyone celebrated as an eminently sensible answer.

Nothing gave the youngest daughter so much pleasure as to hear about the worlds above the sea, and the ways in which they were variously apportioned and administered. She made her old grandmother tell her all she knew of the ships and of the towns (a great deal), of their fortifications and their distribution of resources (very little, but she didn't mind lying). The defining characteristic (or so it seemed to the youngest daughter) of these places was what a great store its peoples seemed to set in declaring one place not another—this country *here* can never be that country *there* and vice versa, and how strictly important the notion of a front door was.

"You mean if someone has something, and I should like to use it, and they don't want me to," she said to her grandmother, "all they have to do is put it behind their front door, and keep it there, and there's nothing I can do about it?"

"Not unless you were willing to get into a great deal of trouble for the keeping of it," her grandmother said.

"But that's unreasonable," she said. "What right has a front door to keep me from anything? My goodness, I keep clams and things out of my garden, but I don't expect them to stop *trying* just because I put a few rocks around it. It's my garden because I till it, not because the world stops trying to grow things at my say-so."

"Nevertheless," her grandmother said, "they set a great store by it, and wouldn't give up their front doors for anything."

"You can't have understood it properly," the girl said.

"Front doors," her grandmother repeated, "they're absolutely mad for them, and their fish are covered in soft scales, and roost in stiff pods of kelp that don't move in the slightest, and scream at one another from their nests all day long, for everything that lives there hates quiet. All day long a hot coal rakes its way across the roof of the world, and all night they freeze as little white maggots peep out all over the sky to watch them."

"It isn't decent," she added, and the general opinion was that she was right.

"Decent or not," the girl said, "I'd like to see it for myself."

"And you will," said her grandmother. "When you're of an age, and your affairs are in order, and you have your family's consent, you may sit on the rocks by the coast and watch the ships go by moonlight. Then you will come home, and you can think about what you have seen."

At last the girl came of an age, and her affairs were in order, and she had the consent of her family tucked under the wallet strung round her waist.

"Now you are grown up," said her grandmother, "and you must let me turn you out so everyone who sees you will know your rank," and she placed ropes of nautilus on her neck and ordered eight solemn oysters to clamp onto her hair.

"But this hurts so," said the girl, who had never suffered before and did not like it in the least.

"I would not hurt you unless I could bear the same thing. You are not being asked to do anything without precedent," said her grandmother, "and no one likes to hear someone talk about their aches and pains. Have the decency at least to be quiet about it."

"All the same," the girl said, twisting her mouth, "I don't believe I should like to suffer again. As a matter of fact, I don't believe I will suffer again at all. Good-bye, for now at least." And with that, she drew herself up and vanished into the blue haze overhead.

The sun had set just before she broke her head into the air. Nearby, a large ship rested on the water. The sea and the sky alike were still and cool, but the surface of the ship seethed in continual motion against the waves. Dark figures crawled all along the rigging with a great shouting and waving of arms. Lanterns had been tipped up all around the deck and stuffed with fire, and pennants flashed from every spar. A lurching, crashing music tipped over the sides of the ship and scattered on the waves so that the girl sputtered and thrust her head back under the water, where everything was blessedly dark and quiet. She swam closer to the cabin windows and looked in through the glass. There she saw a smaller crowd of people, not moving about so wildly as the first, but richly dressed, who smiled at each other and spoke in soft voices.

Among them was a young prince—"for practical purposes, much the same thing as a daughter, at least to *them*," her grandmother had said. His rank was obvious from the deference offered him, despite the conspicuous lack of nautilus and clamshells on his person. He was dark-eyed and solemn, or at least civil, and the girl thoroughly approved of him for it. The celebration was for him; it was the prince's birthday, and they were marking it with tremendous merriment, for they had only a single prince to share among all their people.

The girl remembered what her grandmother had told her: "They aren't made as you or I were made. Here, a king knows exactly the number of daughters—or sons, if he wants any—he needs, and produces them as necessary. They have to go to a great deal more trouble than that if they want to get up more people. And they can make only one or two at a time, which makes for a devil of a time with planning, so that sometimes there are too many, and sometimes not nearly enough, and always there is the question of who they are going to make new people *with*. They can't make daughters as individuals *or* as a body politic, nor bud nor generate colonies, as sensible people do. They have to split off into two first, and commit sexuality against one another. I told you it wasn't decent."

When the prince moved from his cabin to the deck, a terrible shouting came from the sailors gathered there, and more than a hundred rockets shot out across the bow, singeing the sky with such a brightness that the girl could hardly bear to look. She had to bathe her eyes in salt water before she could open them again. When she did, it appeared as if every star in heaven had been wounded, and that they were unspooling themselves into blazing white threads that dripped into the sea. Everything was freezing cold and burning hot all at once. The ship itself was so brilliantly lit that everything onboard seemed lost in half radiance, half shadow. No one seemed in the least bit frightened, and everyone who saw the prince smiled at him. In this way the girl figured he must be lovely, so she smiled at him, too.

It grew late, yet the girl did not take her eyes from the ship, nor from the prince once they had adjusted to the glare. One by one, the lanterns drooped lightless, the music paled, and the ship grew quieter. The sea became restless, and every wave began to hiss foam, but still the girl remained by the cabin windows, bobbing up and down in the water. Then suddenly the deck was no longer quiet; sailors moved in a black line up the mast, seizing at the rigging, but the waves threw themselves to yet greater heights, where they were joined by fat lashings of lightning. The sails were soon swamped, and the ship dove down like a swan, and all of it made for great sport for the girl, who had long been cradled by storms such as these.

At once the sea rushed over the deck, sweeping everyone before it. All around her there was a struggling of limbs and gasping for breath, and the girl felt rather sorry for complaining about the weight of a few oysters, now that she could see how thoroughly everyone around her suffered. "I won't complain about them next time," she promised herself.

Now and again she had to swim slightly out of her way to avoid the scattered side effects of the shipwreck. It became so dark she could imagine herself on the seafloor, but then a flash of lightning threw the scene into relief, and she glimpsed the prince sinking below the waves. She brightened at the thought that soon he would be down in her father's country, where she might show him her garden and explain her philosophy of relative value and effective stewardship. *After all,* she thought, *better for him to join us than for us to join him, if he is the only administrator his father has, as having one is scarcely better than having none at all.*

Then she remembered that humans could live only under the strictest of conditions, that their lungs were quite useless when wet, so that by the time he reached her father's house he would be quite dead and unable to learn anything about her philosophies at all, much less help implement them. So he had better not drown.

She dove among the beams of the ruined ship, and found him drifting a few lengths below, tangled in a bit of sail. His eyes were closed, and he seemed not to take a bit of interest in the goings-on around him (for there was still a great deal of thrashing going on just under the waves). The girl, being fair-minded, was careful not to attribute this to indifference and so did not hold his lack of curiosity against him, but tucked him squarely under her left arm and made for shore, mindful that his head faced upward. It was a generally clumsy and inefficient form of travel, but like any good administrator, she never held anyone responsible for their natural limitations.

The prince remained similarly useless once they reached the shore, and since his head seemed determined to loll about on his neck, she was compelled to steady him with one hand on either side of his face. His eyes still did not open, but his mouth hung slack, so she closed it.

"You're very quiet," the girl told him. She frowned meditatively. "I don't mind it. You may kiss me, if you like." The prince said nothing at all to that, so she kissed his forehead, and pushed back his damp hair, and kissed him again. The prince's assets—silence, introspection, slowness to judgment, pliability—all spoke of good breeding and more than compensated for his lack of seaworthiness. He also had, it seemed, the quality of Loveliness—*Or, at least,* the girl thought, *is recognizably lovely to others of his own kind when he is awake,* which was much the same thing.

Soon the morning had scrubbed both storm and ship clean from the horizon, and still the prince's eyes did not open. She had never seen anyone who lived above water so placid before. It seemed eminently sensible, and so she decided to love him for it. She was delighted that she had been away from home less than a day and already she had found something useful to do.

Considering further delay unnecessary, the girl dove back into the sea and tucked herself just beneath the waves, so that she might not have to see him wake up. A little farther down the shore was a long, low building, and a number of people surged out of its doors onto the sand and busied themselves about the prince. One of them sank next to him and pressed his hand tenderly; he soon opened his eyes and sat up, and the activity on the beach consequently increased. When she saw the prince disappear behind the front doors of the building, the girl considered him unlikely to drown again, so she swam farther out into the waves, flipped over neatly, and made for home.

She had kissed him, and she had kept his lungs from getting wet; this made him hers according to the laws of most commonsensical people. It certainly made him more hers than anyone else's, which meant there was a great deal to attend to before she was ready to challenge any front door's claim on him.

Everyone at home made much of her return, and she let herself be fussed over with patient indifference.

"If human beings are not drowned," said the girl to her grandmother once she had been thoroughly scrubbed and fêted, "can anything else kill them? Are they like sea grass, or like seals? Will the same one return again if I yank it up by the roots, or will it die?"

"Humans die," said the grandmother, "and humans suffer too, for they lead short lives and when they are dead, no one eats them. They are stuffed in boxes and hidden in the dirt, or else set on fire and turned into cinders, so no one else can make any use of them; they are a prodigiously selfish race and consider themselves their own private property even in death."

"The prince would never be so miserly as to deny himself to any fellow citizen, whether he is living or dead, I am sure," the girl said, "for I could never love anyone who was not civic-minded, and I am very sure that I love him."

"That's all very good," her grandmother said, "but if he is to make his home here, you must make him promise to let us eat him when he is dead, as you and I will be eaten."

"I am sure that he can be persuaded," the girl said. "He was very persuadable, when I fell in love with him. You know he is the only prince they have at all up there; he has no sisters or colleagues to share his burden or offer him advice. It is a singular place, and everyone seems quite determinedly alone, and I think he will be grateful to learn there are more reciprocal ways of living."

"They are powerfully ungenerous," her grandmother agreed. "They do not think of the future, as we do; each one keeps a little soul all locked away for himself, and once their bodies are used up, their souls go off somewhere no one else can reach and continue along in perfect isolation forever and ever."

"But what a terrible *waste* that must be," cried the girl. "I can think of a dozen better things I could do with a soul."

"More's the pity that you haven't got one, for I have no doubt you could put a soul to a great deal of good use."

"I should like to get a soul," said the girl. "The prince has one already. I might have his. I have put my mouth on his mouth, and surely that counts for something, even among savages."

"Getting a soul takes suffering and solitude," said her grandmother. "We are much better off than they are, no matter how much they squander their birthright."

"I've suffered already," said the girl. "Not much, perhaps, but I should still like to get *something* for my suffering."

"You could," said her grandmother, "if the prince were to love you such that his own people were nothing to him, and if he forgot the two parents who made him, and if all his thoughts were yours, and if he were wed to you with his full heart, then his soul could become yours, and you would gain a share in his eternity."

The girl thought of the prince, quiet and still on the

sand with his dark eyes closed, and she thought about gaining something from him. She considered his soul quite her own already, minus a few necessary formalities.

The very next day the girl swam out from her father's house to visit the sea-witch. *She* didn't call her a sea-witch, obviously, because people who live there don't go around affixing the word "sea" to everything any more than you would speak of visiting your land-doctor or your dirt-grocer. She didn't call her a witch either, as a matter of fact, but no translation is perfect, and for our present purposes, there's not much more you need to understand about the sort of person the sea-witch was. After all, it *was* true that she lived in the sea, and it *was* true that she could make things happen that other people couldn't. She was a very effective and useful person, which meant, as far as the girl was concerned (although, you will remember, that you would never call her a girl, if you got a good look at her), a sea-witch was just another sort of king's daughter.

Now here is what the sea-witch looked like: she was hinged neatly in the middle; she could jump very high by bending and straightening her great-foot; she could whistle water through her teeth and hit a swimming fish one hundred yards away; and she had no head at all. She was lovely to look at.

And here is what the sea-witch's house looked like: it was composed of a hundred white chimneys that shot out merry little clouds of particulate all night and day. The chimneys were crusted in mottled bits of iron and long drips of sulfide and flanked with lovely pale calcium blooms. Out of this smoking corridor grew tube worms, which the sea-witch tended herself, and which had no faces at all, only pale, slender midguts and foreguts that concluded in a red mouth that danced in the current. The mouths turned and followed carefully everything that swam by. The sea-witch's home was bounded by a dead brine pool and old dripping waterfalls, and a soft shower of marine snow was always pattering lightly against the roof of her chimney-palace. It was too hot and too cold and too wriggling for anyone else to live there, so the sea-witch owned it. She turned it out quite neatly, too.

The girl felt the worms twitching underneath as she swam, mouthing at her limbs softly as she passed over. She went faster until she came to a chimney that would have looked to you like a squat stone beehive—it didn't look like a beehive to *her*, but what *she* thought it looked like wouldn't mean anything to you. Anyhow, it was in this chimney that the witch lived, and so it was this chimney that the girl came to.

"Good day and well-met, girl," said the witch, spitting a long stream of nacre on the floor in welcome. "Come in, then, and bring your business with you."

"Good day and thanks, Mother," the girl said (who was polite as well as efficient). "I'm off to get a soul, and a prince besides, if I can manage it."

"Can't see what need you have for one," the witch said. "What will you do with it?"

"Oh, I haven't got any plans, exactly," the girl said. "Only I'm good at figuring out what to do with things, and the ones that have the things to begin with don't seem interested in putting them to use, just in keeping them where they already are."

The witch nodded, or made an approximate gesture that involved folding and unfolding herself quickly. "I can't abide selfishness either, an it comes to that. Well, good luck to you, and if you manage to bring either one back, I'll look forward to a good meal in your company. But better a plate of herbs where love is than a stalled ox and hatred therewith." (The witch didn't say "ox," or "love" either, if it comes to that, but there are other books that better explain that sort of thing. Hadn't you better be reading some of them?)

The witch looked the girl up and down with a critical eye. (You know, by now, I think, that the witch *had* no eyes, and I need not explain every little difference to you, but bear in mind that even if someone is merely in possession of a clot of photosensitive cells and a rudimentary sort of lens that is only dimly aware when a shadow passes overhead, they might be just as proud of that clot of cells and that rudimentary lens as you are of your own two eyes.)

"You'll need a great deal more skin than you've got now," she added, "and you'll be dried out all over, and you'll get two limbs on the top half of you and two on the bottom and no more than that, and if you lose one, that's the end of it. There's no growing *those* back; no one up there abides by the blessed mandate of Radial Symmetry. Cut one of them in half—in either direction!—and they just fall apart stupidly, never to move again."

"That will be novel," the girl managed to say, although she looked more than a little pale at the prospect of losing Radial Symmetry, which she had been catechized in from her earliest memory.

Then the witch laughed so loud that she fell to the ground and wriggled about. "I will prepare a drink for you, with which you must swim to land tomorrow before sunrise, and sit on the shore and drink. All manner of things will happen to you: you'll grow a hard plate of bone that will split the vaults inside your head; two soft cysts to force the air out of your chest; sprout studs of bone all in a line down your back; you will be mammalized, and it will hurt, and it will hurt until you are back here with all of us, in your own form again. But all who see you will consider you lovely, and you will be able to open your eyes wide against the sun. If you can bear this, then I can help you."

"I can bear this," the girl said. "Most likely," she added, for she had never actually had to bear anything as yet and was only guessing.

"Well, I'll give it you, then," said the witch, "but you *should* be careful, because I don't know much about the undoing of it, and once you've become human all over—instead of just partway, as you are now, and might I say, I like your present form much better—you might become particularized and believe you belong to yourself only, instead of in the normal way—you belonging to all of us and we all to you—and never return to the water, or your sisters, or your father's house, or mine. And if you were to fail in winning the prince or his soul, if he were to join with another or hoard his own soul to himself, then you might die, and turn into nothing useful at all, and I should have wasted an afternoon, and gone hungry to boot."

"Just the same," the girl said, "I don't think I'll fail."

"Another thing," said the witch. "I can't do voices. I mean that I can't make you a new mouth that makes sounds. Not the kind *they* could understand, anyhow. I can make you a mouth that can suck in air and blow it back out again, and a mouth that can eat the right kind of food and swallow it, but I can't make a mouth that can do all that *and* put a voice in it, too. So you won't have one."

It was a disappointment, but like any good administrator, the girl never held anyone responsible for their natural limitations. "No voice, then," she agreed. "I'll make up the difference somehow." It was getting to be a great deal of trouble for a single prince, but there *was* a great deal to be said for doing something unprecedented.

At any rate, everything happened exactly as the witch said it would; the girl beached herself in the dark, drank from her little cup, experienced a fair bit of discomfort as her skeleton made itself known in new and distressing configurations, tested out her voice, found none, and assessed the situation, along with her assets (alive, conscious, in possession of a singleness of purpose, also in possession of eyelids) and disadvantages (unable to change color, one-way joints, a sudden and profound sense of isolation). Then the sun came up. The prince was there, which was remarkably convenient.

His eyes were so fixed upon her that she decided she must have uncommonly attractive legs, or else somehow the principle (if not the reality) of Radial Symmetry was visible in her new form. She found, somewhat to her surprise, that she was rather put off by his obvious approval, given how much trouble she had gone to just to split so much of herself apart. He had not, it had to be said, *asked* her to suffer this for him, and so could not strictly be blamed, but she found herself doing it just the same.

The prince asked her who she was and where she came from, and she looked at him with not a little disgust, that he did not know her. *No point in suffering for someone who hasn't asked you to do it,* the witch had said, *but please yourself;* he *won't recognize what pain looks like on your face, that's for certain.* He evidently couldn't recognize disgust, either, taking it for a softer emotion and guiding her inside a nearby building. She couldn't help feeling, even in the midst of everything, a little thrill at the prospect of stepping through her first front door. She walked through it as easily as anything, although every step she took was as painful as promised.

As far as all that goes: the girl was not from the sort of people who took much interest in cataloguing various types of pain. Nor would she be interested in the sort of person who *was*, chiefly because knowing more about something one cannot change is not especially useful. So as far as the girl was concerned, things either hurt, or they didn't, and you could either make them stop hurting, or you couldn't. Walking hurt, and the sun boiled hot and furious over the horizon every morning, and the food she ate was bloodless and dry and made her stomach twist up, but she couldn't help any of that, and that's all there was to say about it.

At any rate, she couldn't say anything about the pain, and so no one noticed, least of all the prince, who brought her home with him in a careless sort of way, and covered her in clothes and smiled at her and gestured broadly at a small stuffed sort of bed that was evidently meant for her use and not to be shared. He seemed to have a frenzy for clothes shared by all members of the administration; the girl could scarcely walk from one room to the next without being frantically presented with clothes by someone or other.

It was strange, the girl thought, that the prince had not yet bothered to thank her for coming to see him, for rearranging her skin, for all the suffering she was enduring for him, simply because he had not asked her to and did not know why she did it. It seemed to her that he was much nicer when he had been drowned and his eyes were closed, but that did not make her love him any less. He simply had a great deal to be taught.

The prince kept her near him at all times, and was

forever tipping her chin up with his two longest fingers, as if he remembered having his face pointed to the sky as she swam him to shore. Her little stuffed bed sat just inside the door to his own room, and she slept when he slept, like a favorite dog. Where he went, she went, but never to assist or facilitate, merely to attend.

There had been plenty of activity at the beginning over whether the girl could speak, or was planning on it anytime soon, or whether she should be *made* to speak, or if she belonged to anyone (which she considered a ridiculous question, as she belonged to *everyone*). She expressed no preference one way or the other, and eventually she was left alone about it. They did not seem anxious to find a purpose for her. She was not going to be useful, she was not going to be shared, she was not even going to be eaten. It was with mounting horror that she realized their selfishness extended even to her.

She took to sneaking out of her bed after everyone else had gone to sleep and taking the steps that led down to the sea, where she could bathe her feet in salt water and think about her old garden. Once during the night, her sisters came up linked arm-in-arm, chorusing reproachfully at her from the water, and she tried to tell them how severely she had overestimated her ability to make something constructive out of suffering—but she had the wrong sort of mouth, and no voice to tell them with. They waved at her anyhow, and told her of all the work they had been undertaking, and promised to come again.

After that, they came to the same place every night, and she threw crusts of bread for them to eat, and their bright hair flashed in the lamplight as they lunged to snatch it from the waves with their teeth. After she ran out of bread they would bob around sullenly until she spread her arms wide in apology. Then they would vanish.

As the days passed she caught herself clinging to the prince more often, and his arms went easily around her, but it never entered his head to forget the two parents who made him, or to make all his thoughts her thoughts, or to wed her with his full heart, or give any part of his soul to her, which was exceedingly frustrating.

Sometimes the girl would look at him very hard, and try to ask "Do you not love me yet?" with her eyes, and she thought if she had any luck at all, he would begin to find her necessary. She had no luck at all, and began to despair of her plan entirely.

So she began instead to consider how to minimize her losses, capitalize on her assets, and make a strategic retreat. She did not blame the prince—he was not to blame for her limitations—but she began to think about how she could love him more efficiently. It so happened that very soon the prince had to marry, which was a great relief to the girl, who was beginning to wonder whether the leadership of his country cared about the perpetuation of daughters in the slightest. Then it was said that the particular daughter of a particular neighbor was to be the bride. This struck the girl as unnecessary—why favor specificity over proximity?—but as she was merely a guest and had not been invited to comment upon their cultural practices, she kept her own counsel. The prince still tipped her chin up with his two longest fingers, but now did so distantly, as if something had changed.

A ship was prepared, and all the favorite members of the court were put on it, and they wobbled cautiously out over the sea, hugging the coastline for three days. The morning they sailed into the bride's harbor they were greeted by bells and gunfire and cheering, as if the wedding was something that was going to happen to everybody instead of merely two people.

The bride was brought forth, and the girl had not had time to form an opinion of her before the prince was married. She decided she could love the bride just as easily as she had loved the prince. A fanciful sort of person waved censers about, and the prince and the bride clasped their hands together, and the girl held up the bride's train. Once again she saw lamps being flung up in every corner; once again rockets disemboweled themselves in a rush to produce light, although this time she could watch without fear of being blinded.

Then there was a great deal of laughter, and dancing, and motion. The prince never left off putting his fingers all over his bride's face. Nor could his bride decide for what purpose she had a mouth; one moment it was crammed with food, the next moment it was smeared against some part of the prince. Eventually the two disappeared into the bridal cabin, and everyone left without milled around aimlessly. The crowd bled members belowdecks until eventually no one was left above but the ship's automated operator at one end and the girl at the other.

The girl leaned against the edge of the railing and looked out over the sea for signs of morning. She saw a group of her sisters rising out of the water, their heads quite naked, for they had cut off all their hair.

"Hello again," they said, "finding you has been awfully tiresome, and we're very eager to go home. Are you ready to go home? We've brought you a knife, in case you are ready to come home, unless you'd rather die up here and be burnt into ashes. Take it, and visit the prince with it, and let his blood coat your feet, and let them grow back together, and have a sensible body again. The grandmother misses you, and your garden is just wild with polyps, and the witch says never mind about the meal, that she isn't hungry for anything but to see you home again. All our hair is gone. We gave it to the witch so she could make a knife with it. Well, what have you to say to that?" Then they all sighed deeply and mournfully, for they were not used to making such long speeches.

The girl tilted her head and waved cheerfully down at them. Then she bound her hair at the back of her neck, pulled her legs back up from the edge of the ship, and disappeared inside the cabin.

The girl drew back the curtain covering the marriage-bed, and saw the prince sleeping against his bride's chest.

She bent down and kissed his brow, then hers, and then his, then hers once again for good measure. It would be too bad to have suffered so without getting the prince for it, but now it was his and his bride's turn to suffer. Since the girl had already done her suffering cheerfully, she saw no reason why they should complain either. The knife jumped a little in her hand, and then it jumped first in the prince's throat, then his bride's, and a red line trailed after it. Then the girl flung the knife into the sea.

"Oh, that's lovely," she said, and she found that she had a voice again, and that she was not suffering in the least. "That's so much better. That's *wonderful*." She wriggled her toes around in the blood and left scrunched-up little footprints behind her as she returned to the railing.

"Hello, sisters," the girl called out as she waggled her bloody legs over the side. "Oh, but it's a relief to see all of you. I can't begin to tell you the extent of my troubles. I'm covered in little fissions—or fissures, I misremember which is which, but I'm split all over like a reef—and I can only move in four directions, none of them interesting, and I don't care if I never see another soul as long as I live. I want to come home, and be around sensible people, and dig up my garden, and never have to look at the sun again."

Then she looked down to see that she had been fully restored to herself, flexing joyfully in every direction, and found her body just as it had been, and she loved the prince and his bride better than she ever had before.

"I'm coming, sisters," she said, and she felt three voices

humming all at once in her throat—her own, and the prince's, and the prince's bride (*her* prince, now, and *her* bride, too). And she had two souls inside her, and they both belonged to her, and she smiled, and she slipped back into the sea.

TWO

The Thankless Child

AFTER EVERY MEAL CAME THE INVOCATION TO Combat Ungratefulness. All three girls had been catechized in the simple prayers that preceded the salt-ration years earlier but for a long time were without a godmother to chant the clarification. Meals were always taken outside, weather permitting, and only once the sun had gone down, with their godmother alone on one side of the low stone table in the garden. The girls sat on the other side, whomever had finished her work the soonest seated closest to the head.

This had been the order of things: Paul, the eldest, had a dead mother who had been reduced to salt a decade since. The bones had been gathered in a square of fabric, bundled neatly, and buried at the northwest end of the family grounds; a false cypress, which was not by the strictest definition a tree but an overgrown shrub, grew over them, and dropped fat pale spiders from its branches. After an appropriate but not elaborately drawn-out mourning period, Paul's father was taken husband again, and produced her sisters in quick succession. Gomer and Robin were equally black-eyed and charming, quick with both work and a smile, handsome of face and of person, less eager to please than universally pleasing.

Gomer and Robin's mother had no training in the motherly arts and confined herself to matters of business and household management. Their father knew the primary psalms, his place, and not much else. The godmother had appeared on the day of Gomer's baptism and supplied the family with water she had conjured herself to mark the occasion. She joined the household as godmother and doctrinal master that same evening. Gomer, who had little native interest in religion but a placid desire to be generally approved of, took to her godmother at once. Robin took to her too, although with none of Gomer's innate placidity; Robin created the unique impression of always seeming to be on the verge of spilling something on herself, despite not being in the least bit clumsy. Paul's comparative reserve could not help but draw the godmother's attention, and Paul was often the worse off for it.

The godmother could read, and write a little when the situation called for it; she could walk in the noonday sun without fainting; commission deacons; haggle with the grocer; perform minor miracles; turn a dog into a man for upward of three hours; cast out territorial spirits; slaughter a chicken without spilling a drop of blood; initiate mysteries; and she could name over one thousand neurotoxins. She made all her own clothing, and the children's too, and she was neither bent nor stooped with age. The garden, since she began to tend to it, produced both onions and cabbage and several other eatable things beside, and no birds ever landed in it.

"Receive all things," the godmother began. "Bless all things, mind all things; guard against ingratitude and the waste of water. Build your seat on a high place and watch for thieves; mind in what manner, when, whence, how many, and what kind come to break in and steal. When the watch grows weary, stand up and enter into the guard of the mind, then sit down again and attend to the task." She turned her head to Paul. "What is it to be grateful, girl?"

"To be grateful is to be wakeful and watchful," Paul said. "To be grateful is to remember. To be grateful is to acknowledge one's lawful debts and keep a balanced ledger."

"Attend, and affirm, the reasons you are grateful to me," the godmother said. "Eldest first."

"For my life," Gomer said. "For my going out and my lying down. For your right hand, which holds me fast. For my eyes, my ears, my limbs, and my senses. For the clothes on my back, the salt in my hand, the water-storage tanks in my home, the walls that keep out lawbreakers, for the rain when it comes, for the knowledge of the word you have given me."

"It is sufficient," said the godmother. "Full salt and full rations for tomorrow." Gomer's flush broke through the dirt on her face, and she smiled broadly as she twisted her hands under the table, as if wringing out every last drop of the compliment.

Robin came next, reciting in a high, practiced voice: "For consolation, for comfort, for the discernment between what can be eaten and what not ought to be eaten, for the power to keep the dead in the ground, for your commandments, for your wonder-working, for the knowledge of poisons and of proofs, for the safety of your garden in a wicked world."

"It is sufficient," said the godmother. "Full salt and three-quarters rations, for failing to mention the watch-fires I have set around this house that burn both day and night."

Paul said nothing, and the godmother did not ask her to speak. She sat on the lowest stool at the end of the table, for her work had taken her to the farthest ends of the property, and she had been late in presenting herself to the house. She had broad shoulders and reddish-brown hair, which she wore very short. She sat at the end of the table six nights out of seven.

"Attend, and account how you love me," the godmother said. "Youngest first."

"More than eyes," Robin said. "More than life, more than health, more than salt-rations and true water, more than breath, more than honor; you are speech and liberty to me."

"More than milk," Gomer said. "More than eggs, more than a portable generator, more than bread and lamps, more than my living parents and my own sweet bed; you are air and light to me."

"Paul, I will not ask how you love me," said the godmother, "as I know that you do not." Gomer twisted her hands under the table again, but said nothing. Robin looked at Paul out of the corner of her eyes and pulled her mouth to one side, but said nothing. Paul stacked her sister's dishes under her own and swept the crumbs off the table onto the ground.

"Sly," said the godmother to Paul's sisters. "Sly and secret and workful, and gives her loyalty to a dead woman even as she neglects the living woman who stands before her. She wastes water and salt weeping over those who neither notice nor profit from them. Look, she has been crying today; her eyes betray her."

Paul still said nothing, having long since learned better than to offer a defense. Soon enough the godmother gathered up her cup and book and, rising from her seat, led them all in the final salt-prayer.

"Blessed be salt. Blessed be the solution, from water and from rock, intervener in the blood.

"Blessed be the anti-caking agent, the de-iced high-way. Guard against the seizure and the fluid of the lungs.

"Blessed be the Trace Elements. You iodize all things, preserve all things, desiccate the living and the dead, the Great Solubizer.

"Blessed be Potassium, salt's glorious spouse, guardian of the concentration gradient, protector of resting potential.

"Let my flesh be a safeguard of the reserves: let my body preserve the salt for those who will come after. Bless the rations. Bless the Alberger process. Keep us from the daily minimum, the saltless fits. May she who wastes salt, lose salt; may she who finds salt, keep salt.

"Salt within me, salt before me, salt behind me, salt beneath me, salt to my left and to my right, salt when I lie down, salt when I sit down, salt when I arise, salt in the heart of all who think of me, salt in the mouth of all who speak of me, salt in every eye that sees, salt in every ear that hears."

With that the meal was over, and they went inside.

* * *

Gomer and Robin attended to their own rooms, their own laundry, and their own labor. Their mother managed the house's income and expenditures; their held-in-common father handled all responsibilities municipal and civic. Paul was responsible for the kitchen, the guardroom, the chapel, the compost heap that fed the garden, the neatening of the family pathways, the tithe, and the several public rooms of the house, because, as the godmother had pointed out, "Paul has a dead mother, who does no work, and so her daughter must work for both."

What had happened, what had always happened, was this: Paul's work took her often to the false cypress that flourished over her mother's bones at the end of the field. There were no other trees nearby (although it was *not* a tree, precisely, but a shrub, no more than six feet in height and perhaps eight feet around), which meant it provided the only shade to be found for half a mile during the worst heat of the day. It was not for emotional but logistical reasons that Paul preferred it. Had there been another option, she would gladly have availed herself of it, for the shade the false cypress provided was patchy and thin, and she had to thrust herself underneath its branches in order to hide herself from the sun, and cover her face with her hands, as bloated yellow spiders rained softly down on her. If she cried sometimes as she lay underneath, that was an expected physiological reaction. If her mother's tree sometimes responded sympathetically, that was to be expected, too. Her mother had been in possession of not-insignificant sympathetic powers, and if every so often a spare bundle of nails or scrap of ash-soap or loaf of bread dropped down with the spiders, Paul did not waste them.

That evening, Paul was using her mother's soap to scrub the dishes in her sink and was up to her elbows in foam when the godmother appeared in the doorway. Paul briefly dropped one knee in the lightest possible genuflection without releasing the dish in her hand.

"When you need something next," the godmother said, "you do not go to *her*. You will come to *me*."

Paul shrugged. "It is no concern of yours, I think," she said. "I have rejected nothing from you, nor sought any of her favors. What I am given, I use, and give thanks for it, as you have taught me."

For a moment the only sound in the kitchen was the light splashing of Paul's hands in the sink. Then the godmother was at her elbow, spilling a low and steady stream of words in her ear.

"You cannot continue to take from the dead without incurring a debt you cannot possibly pay. My yoke is easy, and my burden is light; the yoke of the dead is not so easily thrown off. What you need, I will provide. No one else."

"You do provide for me," Paul said. "I seek nothing from her but shade at noon, and yet I cannot turn away a gift given unasked."

"Then you do not *love* me," the godmother cried. "You do not love me, and I have loved you with my whole and living heart from the first day I mothered you, and I will perish for the want of you."

The godmother plunged her hand into the sink and groped blindly until she found Paul's fingers, and clutched at them. "You will kill me," she said again. "Have I not given you more than your sisters, although you love me less? Have you not the privilege of sharing my own bed? Do I not appoint you in the best clothes, the first pair of new shoes, the best tools, the first choice of food, when you have earned food? Who else's hand would I clasp against my own? Who else have I offered my heart to but you? Yet you spurn it, and offer me stares, and dawdle in the fields rather than sit at my honored side at table. If I thought it would bring a smile to your face, I would let myself slip underground like your first mother, to have you willingly climb under my branches, to know you love me."

Paul let her hands go slack under the water. "I love you," she said, and the godmother clasped her all the harder, stroking between each knuckle with her long fingers.

"How do you love me?" the godmother said. "How can one be so young, so lovely, and so unfeeling?"

"I will come to you," Paul said. "I will come to you for everything."

The godmother smiled in great triumph, and her fingers encircled Paul's wrists tightly. "And you will bring me the gifts she gives you? Not hoard them to yourself? Not drive me off, as some stranger unfit to share your joy?"

"I will bring you everything."

"Not to come to me," the godmother said, "suggests you are not prepared to be grateful to me. It smacks of ingratitude. Am I not your proper godmother? Is not my power sufficient? There is nothing I would not give you, if you would only acknowledge my right to grant you favors. What is it that I ask of you, that you find so impossible? What have I only ever asked of you?"

"To be good," Paul said. "To be a good girl, a good daughter, and to return your love honorably." The god-mother looked at her with a long and searching look, and nodded, and broke her hold, and shook her hands dry over the soaking-water.

The godmother handed her a dish from the drying rack. "This is dirty. Clean it again." Paul thrust it back into the sink and scrubbed again, then handed it back for inspec-tion. The godmother swiped it with the dishcloth that hung from her belt and stacked it neatly with the others.

"Everything you need, I will provide," the godmother said again. "All I ask of you is to love me and to be good. Are you prepared to meet those terms?"

"I am prepared," Paul said, and allowed herself to lean a little against the edge of the sink.

"You need salt," the godmother said—it was not a question—and flashed something small and white in her hand. Paul shook her head and pressed her lips together.

"You have been crying," the godmother said in her most businesslike tone, "and have been at half rations for nine days. Your head aches, and you cannot eat, and you are clutching at the sink to stay upright."

Paul nodded, and in an instant the godmother's hands flew to Paul's face, one at her throat and one on her lips. Paul felt the familiar prickle on the back of her tongue, and tried to swallow. The hand at her throat stroked gently downward as she gulped and heaved over the sink. "I can't," she said, gasping, and then there was a glass of water at her lips and a hand in her hair, and she accepted both gratefully. Finally she swallowed, and felt the prickle blossom into a hot, hysterical pool in her stomach.

"Are you going to be sick?" the godmother asked, brushing the back of her hand over Paul's forehead. "Shall I fetch a bucket?"

"No," Paul said, and shook her head tightly. She straightened up and kept her hands close at her side. "No, I'm not going to be sick."

"Are you quite all right now?" the godmother said, and her voice was gentle.

"Yes," Paul said. "I'm sorry. I'm all right now."

* * *

It did not happen that the members of the parish gathered together often; there were monsters on the earth in those days. But the priest's son was in need of a wedding, and the neighborhood offered up their children for his selection.

The girls' father had called it a public concern, reminded them the family had never balked at civic participation, and left it at that. Gomer and Robin's mother had calculated their bridewealth in both directions the day they were baptized and determined that whether they went as grooms or as maids, the budget would abide. So they were all right to go, if they liked, and both decided they *would* like.

"Gomer might bathe, for a change," Paul said over the

washtub to her sisters the afternoon they had been granted ordinary leave. "There's plenty of room with the laundry; jump in and take a bath, if you think you can stand the shock."

"And resign my wife to a lifetime of disappointed hopes, dreaming always of the day I take another?" Gomer said. "Thanks just the same, but he'll have to be clean enough for both."

"You'd wife him, then?" Paul said.

"What, catch me volunteering for anything more than husband's work?" Gomer said. "He's a priest's son, he can already read, and anyhow I'm too old to train in anything new. No, I'll go unwashed and husband both, or I won't go at all."

Robin looked more shocked than usual, which took some doing. "It would be presumptuous," she said, "to assume yourself husband, when you do not know their household's need—when our own mother has set a perfectly good example of finding a role that suits her talents, rather than making demands of—"

"I rather wonder, Robin," Paul said, "at your eagerness to follow her good example, as it is no secret that you'd scrape up the dust with your heels and crow like the Devil if our godmother told you it held the key to mastering the mothering arts."

There was silence for a minute, then Paul spoke again. "What an interesting game you've found, Robin, alternating your mouth between open and closed so quickly. I wonder what it's called, and if anyone can play?"

"Spoken like a true wife," Gomer said, laughing, and after a minute Robin found it in herself to laugh, too.

The seat by the fire had been empty, and then it was not; the godmother did not fuss about making her appearances now that the girls had grown and ceased to be overcome with delight by the many secret ways she knew to enter a room.

"How much joy you find in thinking which of you will leave me first," she said, writing something unintelligible with her finger in the ashes on the hearth, "which of you will take your strength and add it to another family, and diminish the power of mine. I wonder if you have ever thought of bringing someone to me, of joining their strength with ours? Perhaps not. You will notice, of course, that your father has granted you leave, and your mother has granted you leave, but *I* have granted you nothing, nor indeed has my leave been sought."

Gomer was the first to her feet, genuflecting so earnestly she quite lost her balance and had to reestablish herself against the table. Robin followed suit, a little less desperately, and remained frozen mid-droop until the godmother nodded her acknowledgment. Paul kept at the washtub.

"See how Paul doesn't greet me," the godmother said sadly to the ashes on the hearth. "Paul, Paul, you are careful and troubled about many things, yet only one thing is needful. Your sisters have chosen that good part, and it will not be taken away from them."

"Luke ten, forty-one and forty-two," Robin said, but no praise was forthcoming, and she sat back down.

"The mangler is electric," Paul said without looking up, "and I know you don't want us running out the generator."

"Let me mind the generator," the godmother said. "You mind your manners and look at me."

Paul did, and grinned a little as she felt the familiar tug against her own mind as she caught her godmother's hopeful eyes. "Godmother," she said, and swept a leg slowly behind her.

"Mind your labor" was all the godmother said, and Paul returned to her laundry.

"We would not go without your permission," Gomer said. "That was never our intention."

"Remember your baptism and do not lie," the godmother said. "You mock me in my own home and make plans to leave it. But the journey could be quite difficult, I should think. A journey to the priest's house could be quite impossible, if it were undertaken without permission and without blessing to guard the walk. Fire, what do you think?"

The fire went out quite suddenly, throwing the room into blackness and smoke. Robin, who could never manage her response to anything, squealed aloud, and Gomer choked out something that might have, if one were feeling generous, been described as a cough.

After a moment, a scrap of flame reappeared over the hearth, and the godmother's face was wreathed in lights. "I am not unreasonable," she said. "Make an act of contrition, and you can go with my blessing."

Gomer and Robin, on both their knees, declared they were heartily sorry for having offended her, and detested all their shortcomings because of her just punishments, but mostly because they had offended her who was deserving of all-love; they firmly resolved, with her help, to err no more and to avoid the near occasion of ingratitude. Paul said nothing. Paul was not allowed to make the same acts of contrition as her sisters; Paul could only ever be forgiven in a manner that was peculiar to herself, which often meant that she went unforgiven altogether.

"Dress yourselves. Attempt to do so without humiliating me" was all the godmother said in response, and they were dismissed, Gomer flinging her roundest eyes over her shoulder at Paul as she went.

"And will Paul go tonight?" the godmother asked. "Will Paul turn wife or husband?"

"I would go," Paul said, "if for nothing else than to see another family's house; beyond that I have no thought."

"Paul will marry," the godmother said. "Paul would marry her own pride, if no one else sought her out."

There was very little Paul could say to that that would not be called a lie, and Paul would rather be called ungrateful than a liar, as long as she had to choose between the two.

"To Paul," the godmother said, drawing herself up from her seat, "who loves her labor above all things, I give an extra gift: more work, and more solitude." She scattered two handfuls of black lentils over the dying fire, until they were mixed in with the ashes. "Pick them all out in an hour, and I will dress you myself." There was a touch on Paul's shoulder. "Mind you do not burn your hands. I could not stand to see them ruined." Then she was gone.

Before Paul could move toward the hearth, two gray pigeons alighted on the kitchen window, cocking their heads this way and that, and jumped down onto the floor, strutting smartly and kicking up their red heels. They moved like heartbeats under the table, and were quickly joined by a pair of turtledoves, then two great black crows, shiny as beetles. Then the sky opened up in a great whirring swarm, and the floor came alive with the mumbling and rustling of wings. The pigeons nodded their heads and surged up to the hearth's edge and began to pick, pick, pick. And the others also began to pick, pick, pick, and Paul could not move for the soft press of feathers against her.

* * *

The godmother had said nothing when Paul had pressed a fist-warm bundle of lentils into her hands, merely wiped the ash away tidily and looked over all three of the girls. Gomer, who still had not bathed, made a concession to the public good and wore her best work clothes, and a new coat over them. Robin's eyes were bright, though it was difficult to tell if this came from anticipation of an unusual event or merely her customary anxiety. They were to keep their eyes to themselves on the walk to the priest's house. They were to speak to no one before they reached the priest's gate. They were to eat and speak once inside as they pleased, and Paul was to be home by matins.

The godmother had kept her word and dressed Paul herself, bringing in three heavily wrapped bundles from the garden and laying them at Paul's feet. The first she muttered over and tapped at before opening. She pulled out a fine white shirt, and carefully laced Paul's arms through it, and fastened each button to the throat. "I have made this for only you," she said in Paul's ear as she fixed the collar. "I have put such power in it, engendered it with such virtue as could make even a stone heart happy."

Paul began to recite the first part of the Invocation to Combat Ungratefulness, but the godmother placed a hand on her chin and searched her face with unsparing eyes. "Not that tonight, love," she said softly. "The mothering-psalm first, before you go."

"Where can I go from your Spirit? Where can I flee from your presence?" Paul said, and swayed backward only a very little. "If I ascend to the heavens, you are there; if I make my bed in hell, you are there also. If I take the wings of the morning, and dwell in the uttermost parts of the sea, even there your hand shall lead me, and your right hand shall hold me. If I say, 'Surely the darkness will cover me,' even the night shall be light around me. The night shines as day, the darkness and the light are both alike to you."

The godmother pointed at the remaining two bundles, which speedily unwrapped themselves. Two bobbing, jerking figures rose up and danced out the front door to the first gatepost, where they swayed brokenly under the lamp-light.

"Follow them to the priest's house," she said. "Let them go first. Do not let them get behind you."

* * *

The priest's son was attentive—and more than attentive, amiable; and more than amiable, kind. He made Gomer laugh twice and kept Robin awake all through dinner. To Paul, he had spoken of fence repair and drought and how to best tend gospel-trees, and smiled as he spoke in his mild and pleasant voice. She found herself unwilling to abandon his conversation, even as Gomer had displayed increasingly concerned faces from across the room as the night wore on. Once she got up to leave, and he said, "Oh, must you? Only I'd rather you didn't," and so she stayed.

It wasn't until well after Night Office concluded that she realized Gomer and Robin were nowhere to be found, that dawn was already smearing itself across the sky, that her face was quite flushed, and that she had made a spectacle of herself. "I am sorry," she said as she dipped her head politely and downed the remaining water in her cup. "I'll go now. I do like you, priest's son."

"I like you too, Paul, who is twice mothered," he said, trying to remain grave. "You might consider marrying me, if you have thoughts of marrying."

"I might," she said, and left her chair. "You might be worth marrying."

There were no bobbing figures waiting for her by the garden gate, and she tore down the path toward home guideless.

"You are late, you are late, you are late," the godmother cried out in a pinched voice as Paul rushed through the door. "I did not fetch up those guides from their sleep to see you come home *late*."

"I am sorry," Paul said.

"Your sisters' feet," the godmother said, yanking at Paul's sleeves, "who hobbled them? Their hopes—who trammeled them, that your clumsy hands might be stuffed threefold with gifts? Who wedged their bloody feet in hobnailed shoes, that you might walk the freer? Who did all this and more for you?"

"You did," Paul said. She did not look at her sisters sitting quietly at the kitchen table, hands hidden in their laps.

"I, I, I," the godmother crowed, and smiled, and settled back down onto her heels. "Who has mothered you better? Who has mothered you else?"

"None have," Paul said.

"Who could marry you better? Who has sought your heart, as I have sought it? Not for an evening, not for a conversation—your heart, whole and dangerous."

"None," Paul said.

The godmother smiled, and pulled again at her sleeves. "Paul does not deserve such fine things to wear," she said to no one in particular. "Paul should not go about in clothes she is not suited for." Paul felt the fabric molt and sag into something loathsomely soft; she *knew* rather than *felt* the press of dead fur against her, and little dead mice peeled from her skin and dropped onto the floor.

* * *

When Paul woke next, she was married and in bed in the priest's house, now hers and her family's, too. The window had been left open, and she could see out over the path leading up to the front door.

She rose up on one elbow and took further stock. The door was open, and the hallway was full of low, earnest voices. Her husband was seated at the desk in the corner and smiled when she looked at him. "You're awake," he said. "You're awake, and you are married to me."

Paul smiled back.

"I've got to confess something," her husband said to her. "I know it's a bit early to be confessing to you, but I figure I ought to get into the habit. I've had your things sent for. I should have waited for you to wake and ask you directly, but I've never had occasion to—ah—wake someone after giving them cause for sleep, and I didn't like to disturb you. I hope you don't mind."

"I don't mind," Paul said, and meant it. "*Te absolvo.*"

"A shriving wife," he said, looking enormously pleased with himself. "Or a shriving husband, if you'd like. I didn't know if you wanted to be a wife or not, so I guessed, but we can still change it. I'm trained for both, if that helps."

"Oh, I don't mind," Paul said again. "I don't mind anything. God, but it's nice out today."

"I know what you mean," he said. "Listen, give me five minutes to finish attending to this, and then let's have a proper fight about which of us gets to be wife. Let's have a *terrible* argument. Practice all the names you're going to call me."

"In five minutes, then," Paul agreed. "Married life certainly is orderly." She looked out the window and saw a black figure struggling over the horizon, resolving itself more clearly with every step through the haze of the day's great heat. At first there was only a head visible over a squirming, flickering mass; gradually the torso solidified and was eventually joined by a pair of legs, as it made its way up the main road. It paused briefly under a great cypress tree, nearly vanishing in the blackness below its branches, then resumed its journey under the sunlight to the front door. Paul did not need to see the figure's face to know it could read, and write a little when the situation called for it; could walk in the noonday sun without fainting; commission deacons; haggle with the grocer; perform minor miracles; turn a dog into a man for upward of three hours; cast out territorial spirits; slaughter a chicken without spilling a drop of blood; initiate mysteries; and name over one thousand neurotoxins. The godmother was terribly useful to any household fortunate enough to hold her. She was going to be a great help to Paul in her new position. Paul was terribly lucky to have her.

Paul bounded out of bed, her face warm and cold by turns, and pressed her hands against her temples. Her lungs seized at nothing, two empty fists in her chest. There was no air in this room, no air in the world. Her arms bloomed all over in hot pinpricks, the insides of her eyelids exploded into dark stars, and somewhere outside those footsteps came closer to her door. "Ah," she cried softly, "I shall be sick, I shall be sick, I shall be *sick*—"

"What is it?" her husband asked, crouching at her feet, pressing cool hands against hers. "What's the matter? Can you speak? Can I bring you water?" Someone near the door slipped out and returned with a glass a moment later. He brought it to her lips, and she drank deeply, and then fixed him with her steadiest smile.

"I'm all right," she said, catching her breath. "I'm sorry, everyone. I'm quite all right now."

THREE

Fear Not: An Incident Log

IN THE BEGINNING, WHEN I WAS FIRST MAKING APPEARances to mortals, most of them died before I could speak the first word of truth. Just from the sight of me—they fell right over. Great burly men and women too, not like the kind you see nowadays. I mean, real antediluvian hulks with chests the size of wine barrels and legs like cedar trunks. Their consciences would seize right up; they were that certain I'd come to find them out. And they'd give up the ghost—practically flung the ghost right at me—rather than listen to a word of what I had to say.

The fear of God is the beginning of wisdom, and the distribution and installation of wisdom is the task with which all powers and principalities have been charged, not excepting myself. *Fear* being the operative word, and not *panic*, which is why most of us have learned to start each incident log with a command like "Fear not," or "Dread not," or "Be thou not dismayed," or some other variation thereof; most people are full of the beginning of wisdom already, and appearing before them without some form of reassurance is liable to result in total system overload, followed shortly by shutdown.

So I didn't get much practice speaking for a while. But the helpdesk agreed that this was through no fault of my own, so I kept getting sent out on jobs until I could find someone who was capable of holding up their end of a conversation.

I didn't look then like I do now. This was before the great cloud with brightness around it and the fire flashing forth continually, before everyone had settled on having four faces and calf feet and burning coals on their lips. People, I have found, have a very keen eye when it comes to forms that resemble their own, and it's better to look as different from a person as you possibly can than to try to re-create one of their appearances. You always end up with a little too much of something, or not enough of another, and most people would rather talk to a four-headed chariot than something that looks almost like them but has one too many mouths or eyes that don't close right.

I am authorized to perform acts of justice, power, and retribution, to deliver messages of comfort and healing. I am also cleared to open wombs, to test the hospitality of human hosts, to drive the chariot of fire, proclaim portentous births, deliver destinies, blind the unbelievers, test the faithful, record deeds in the book of life, feed prophets in the form of either raven or dove, open seals, pour out bowls of judgment, and blow all twelve of the lesser trumpets. I am not authorized to take communion or to deal out death. All the deaths listed in my incident history have been accidents; you can check the tickets. I never wanted to dismay anybody, but people *will* die, no matter how careful you are with them.

The thing about people is that they can only handle a *very* little amount of communion. A bite of flesh and a mouthful of blood and that's it, and even that you have to couch in multiple layers of explanation and things like "sacramental union" so they can understand. They live all alone in their own heads, and shudder reflexively at the prospect of God's imminence. I've seen it. I've seen a man spend all his life praying for union with the divine, only to shrink back and scrabble to return to his own skin once he realizes that the presence of the divine is coming for him, even though there's nothing to be afraid of, which is why it's my job to remind them not to be afraid. Everything is ultimately reconciled to God, so there's no reason to be afraid of anything. Just relax and wait to be reconciled; active participation is not required. Personally, I have never been without the presence of the grace of God.

I was around for a little while before the world was made, and I liked it fine then. I like it fine now, too. The Spirit of God moved over the waters, and I moved over the waters, too. There was nothing for anybody to be afraid of, because we were all in the dark then. All things invisible and form-less moved together, and the heavens were filled with the soft rustling of leathern wings.

Then came order. First the firmament, with little win-dows to let in the rain, and then the underworld thrust under the pillars of the deep, and the earth in between, and the terrible winds that blew over it, so that nothing could grow. This was fine too, but the making of the world caused a great noise that has not stopped resounding yet, and all of us have had a ringing in our ears ever since. The Voice of God, once heard, is not easily unheard. The sun burned the sky by day, and the moon spoiled the darkness by night. I don't mean to make it sound like I didn't like them, only that it was an adjustment.

Then came the things that swarm the waters, and the things that creep under the earth. Then came trees. And all of them received blessings. Then came people, most of whom were later drowned. I don't suppose I'm speaking out of order when I say I think it was right they were drowned. I'm merely agreeing with the official decision. These people were fugitives and wanderers, and they drew marks on their foreheads whenever they had done murder, so that every-one who saw them would know and would leave them alone. They promised seven-fold and seventy-and-seven-fold

vengeance, and flung up insane and shivering towers over
the plains that threatened to crack Heaven. And they lived
so long their hearts grew dizzy within them and their
thoughts became thoughts of treachery and deceit, and the
earth became a smoking furnace. So we drowned them, and
all things were made new, and that was better.

The first one I spoke to who did anything besides drop
dead was this woman Hagar. I had not spoken to the man
Abraham, but I spoke to her, and I said, "Fear not," and for
some reason this time it worked, because she only looked
at me and waited for me to go on. I was so excited that I
could hardly remember what came next, which was that
God had heard the cries of her son, and that she ought to
get up. I didn't *say* anything about the well, but the well was
there, and she saw it, so I as good as told her about it. She
was very happy, and so was Abraham, and Ishmael too,
most likely, and eventually all the promises she was given
came to pass.

Now they are both dead and united with God. It does
not especially matter whether her son died of thirst in the
desert or somewhere else later on, because he is united with
God now, and when you are with God you have *always* been
with God, so it does not matter what has or has not happened to you. I mean, it matters, of course, as all aspects of
what has been planned matter, but it does not matter to *you*,
or at least that's what I've been given to understand from
what I've read. But it was nice to make someone as happy
as I made the woman Hagar, because I had never made any-

one happy before. I had not *intended* to make her happy—
please don't misunderstand. Her happiness was incidental
to the task at hand, but I don't think it was wrong of me to
enjoy the results of my work. At all times, whether they live
or die, whether humans obey or flee, whether they offer wor-
ship or blaspheme, I maintain a strictly professional air. I
have never once been reprimanded for how I comport myself
under the sun.

I would also like to take the opportunity to clear up a
matter that I think has often seemed unclear: We all take
turns at being the Satan. If you are assigned to oppose, to
withstand, to stand up against the people of God, or to level
accusations, or to offer temptation or to take possession, you
have been assigned to contend against your colleagues, and
you take your turn as the Great Adversary with a cheerful
spirit and a right good will. Everyone understands this as
part of the great work, and does not take it personally if we
are periodically at odds. Each of us has spent time in outer
darkness, and we have always come back in.

I don't want to talk very much about the other one, the
brother to Hagar's boy, Isaac, who was *not* killed. People are
very tiresome about that, and very pleased with themselves
for having no stomach for the story, as if they have accom-
plished something significant by preferring life to death, or
for begrudging the things God asks of them. It is not a new
thing, to not wish to die. So they complain, but they do not
listen, when if they would listen, their suffering would be
allayed. And so their suffering continues.

I should add, it was very difficult, in those days, to keep anyone from stretching their sons out on altars and offering them up as burnt sacrifices. I was kept quite busy then. There had been talk of an official demonstration, to remind people that burning sons was not strictly necessary unless explicitly called for and that God did not need to be anticipated. But I've talked about this already more than I meant to. I will confine myself to this: God did not ask of Abraham anything that God was not willing to provide for him.

I had wondered if Abraham might become happy at some point when I spoke to him, as Hagar had become happy, but the incident did not seem likely to repeat itself. I was not disappointed by this, as I was not disappointed when people used to die at the sight of me. I simply logged the event and did my job to the best of my ability. I have never held myself responsible for outcomes.

But what I want to talk to you about now is a misunderstanding—I think the only misunderstanding I have ever suffered. I mean what occurred was misunderstood in an *administrative* sense. I do not claim never to have been misunderstood by the recipients of the messages I have delivered. Such a claim would be impossible to verify, and I would not make it. It concerns the man Jacob, and what happened in the place of Mahanaim, when he went there to see his brother, Esau. I had no instructions about what was to take place between the two of them. My concern was strictly with Jacob, and I had no interest in either aiding or hindering reconciliation. It is my understanding that he divided his party into two camps. I have no idea what happened to either of them, as I was never charged with their keeping.

I was sent to wrestle with him until the breaking of the day. I'd never been sent to wrestle anyone before. I'd never been told to touch anyone before, and I'll admit to you that I shuddered a little at the prospect. In my opinion, you can see the blight in them when you get too close. Maybe that's a little superstitious. I don't mind it so much when they're fully dead, you understand. Something that's supposed to be dead, and is dead, that's no surprise, but there's something about a creature that's *going* to be dead but isn't yet, something that *knows* it's going to be dead and doesn't want to be. I've never liked that. When they're still walking around and looking out of their skulls and you can just *see* the rot and the grave that's coming, I'll admit that unsettles me, and the thought of getting close enough to wrestle one still living, flush from shoulder to hip—I just didn't like it. Well, they've never liked the look of me either. So I call that fair.

But I had done worse things, and anyhow it was only until the break of day, and then I could discharge my duties and go back. I was sent here to wrestle and to release him; whatever else God had in store for him was none of my business. I didn't say anything—I mean, there's not much point in telling a man to "Fear not" only to lunge at him, is there? Half of me expected him to go trembling all over and die before I could even lay a hand on him. I won't say I hoped for that. I would have been relieved, but I won't say I hoped for that. Even if I don't like what's being asked of me, I've never not wanted to do my job. You can check my incident report history. I resolve everything. If things don't work out on an assignment, it's never been because I left my post or failed to do what was asked of me. So I kept my mouth shut and drove my foot down into his kneecap, and we started wrestling.

God was with him as well as with me, I think, because otherwise I just don't see how a person would be able to stand up against me for so many hours. But he did. If I had had kidneys to bruise, they would have been bruised by the end of that fight. He struck his way in immediately and jabbed the heel of his hand into my throat. That was something that had never happened to me. But that's not to say the man was *winning*, mind you. I hadn't been sent there to lose, so I touched him on the left socket of his hip and shoved the whole thing out of joint. He made quite a sound at that, but it didn't stop him from coming at me for more than a minute. It did look funny, though, the way his leg drooped.

The sun was coming up, and I was supposed to check back in with the helpdesk once I was finished, so I said, "Let me go, for the day has broken." But he didn't let me go. I suppose I sort of wished then for the days when people used to die at the sight of me. No, I don't really mean that; those were disorganized times. But it seemed to me that there ought to have been a balance between everybody keeling over dead at my approach and one of my assignments countermanding a direct request. Either way, no one listens to me, and I don't care for that. It's my job to be listened to, after all. I didn't like that he could keep hold of me either. He didn't seem big enough to be able to do it, but I had to admit he had me caught fast.

"I have striven with God—if you are *not* God, as I suspect, you have at least been sent by God, for there is nothing quite right about you," Jacob said, "and I have prevailed." He was breathing quite heavily by then, and I could smell the red in his lungs.

Then he said, "I will not let you go unless you bless me," which I'll admit took me by surprise. Well, I'm not authorized to give blessings like that, and no one had told me to go down and bless him. I was supposed to wrestle with him until the breaking of the day, no more and no less, so I didn't say anything, and I didn't let go of him either. If I'm honest, I suppose I didn't really *want* to bless him at that point. I think I may have been offended.

After a little while had passed, Jacob spoke again. "Please tell me your name." Well, I hadn't been authorized to do that either, even though ordinarily I'm cleared to speak the true names of most things, including seven of the most private names of God. But I didn't believe Jacob had any jurisdiction over me—I still don't—and so I said nothing. And then he said nothing, and I still said nothing, and he didn't let me go, and I didn't let him go, and that went on for quite some time. It grew very tiresome after a while, and he wept and shivered a great deal. Finally he stopped weeping and shivering. I left his body where we had been wrestling, when it was over; presumably he is buried there now, or else in some other place. Ultimately he has been reconciled to God, so there's no point in speculating what other outcomes may have been possible. God reconciles everybody.

You are probably thinking I must have violated some ordinance, as I am not normally authorized to deal out death. I want to make it very clear that I do not believe I have broken any rules, and no one in my chain of command has ever expressed anything other than satisfaction with my methods. I am not rebellious. If I had overstepped my bounds, someone would have said something. I was not authorized to either kill the man or bless him, and so I did neither. He died because he would not let go of me. It is not my fault that a man cannot prevail against a principality and a power. No man ever has. I keep telling them not to be afraid, and they shouldn't be, but nobody ever listens to me; I don't think that's my fault either. Anyhow, that was all a long time ago now.

FOUR

The Six Boy-Coffins

ONCE THERE WAS A LITTLE GIRL WHO TRIED VERY hard not to be born. Her father, the king, and her mother, the king's wife, had six children already—all sons. Together they were happy. As the boys grew and took their first steps from the schoolroom to the field, the king realized that they would someday turn into men. Six sons were one thing. Six men were quite another. A king could love his little children; but what could he do with deep-voiced, straight-backed men? And what could a kingdom do with six kings? (He was thinking, perhaps, of his own brothers.)

So one day, the king said to his wife, "If the next child you bear me is a girl, then let the six others die, so that our wealth need not be divided and that she alone may inherit the kingdom." He tousled the hair of their youngest son, who was called Elyas, and who always sat nearest to him, as he said it. And the king's wife said, "It shall be as you say," because it always was.

"Had my own brothers lived," the king said, "they should certainly have tried to harm our own children and stifle our peace." His own brothers, however, had not lived. It was an important task of kingship, determining when brothers and sons were no longer necessary.

And his wife said it was true, what he said, because it was.

The king ordered six small coffins to be made of yew by the city's finest carpenters, and fitted each with a fine goose-down pillow and clean-smelling wood shavings. Even dead, the boys would be king's sons, and he was unwilling to spare any expense.

He ordered that the boy-coffins be placed all in a line in a high-off room, distant from all other rooms in the castle. He ordered the door locked, and the only key given to his wife, whose chief employment was the production and maintenance of any of the king's children, living or dead.

"Cheer up," the king told his wife. "You may bear me another son yet, and then we won't need the key after all."

After this, at every meal, the king's wife turned aside her plate for the king's dogs. At night she took to walking the halls of the castle in her slippers, so that no one could hear her footsteps, fingering the iron key at the bottom of her dressing-gown pocket and whispering to the not-yet child curved like a scythe inside of her, *"Don't be born, please. Go back, if you can. There is no welcome here; find another door. Don't be born. I cannot mother you, so please don't be born. I would make it up to you, if I could, but I can't, so don't be born. If you love me, as a child should, don't ask me to birth you."*

"The king's wife looks drawn and pale," the king announced over supper, looking her over carefully, "and not at all well."

"I feel fine," the king's wife said. She tore off the crust from her bread and put it in her mouth. It had been so long since she had chewed and swallowed that it lay dead and heavy on her tongue. She smiled with her lips closed. "I feel very well."

"But your health is not only your own now," the king reminded her. "It is our child's, and mine. A queen," he reminded everyone else at the table, "is the foundation a king uses to build a future."

The king's wife was thereafter served all her meals in her room, under the king's jolly supervision. "Eat up, my love," he said, hands folded behind his head. "Check her pockets," he instructed the steward. "Check her napkin and under the table. We'll make sure she fills out yet. My daughter"—*Not yours yet, nor yet a daughter neither*, thought the king's wife—"my daughter must have plenty to eat. She is a king's daughter, and must be afforded the care a king's daughter merits." The king's wife had never been a king's daughter. She was outranked by her belly.

One day, as the king's wife sat outside the locked door on a little stool, her youngest son said to her, "What is in this room?"

"Your father is making new beds for you and your brothers," his mother said brightly. "Lovely new beds for grown-up boys."

"Then why are you crying?" he asked.

"That," his mother said, "I cannot tell you."

But he would give her no peace until she told him. At last she took the key from her pocket and unlocked the door, showing him the six coffins in a row, well glossed and warm to the touch, already filled with sweet-smelling pine shavings.

First she had to explain death to him. Then she explained the rest. "If this child is a girl, you will all be killed and buried together in here."

"Could you try not to have a girl?" Elyas asked.

"I cannot help it," she said.

"Could you try not to have it at all?"

"I have tried," she said. "It is a hard thing to stop, once it has started."

"Could I help you stop it?" he asked, and she fell about his neck and wept for the sweetness of him.

Then he begged her to lay off crying. "We will take care of ourselves," he promised her. "If the child comes, we will run away, and find something less dangerous to be than king's sons."

So his mother gave her son this advice: "Go to the woods with your brothers and find the highest tree you can. Climb it, and keep a watch on this tower every day. When the child comes, I'll contrive to raise a flag out the window—white if it is another boy and safe for you to return. Red if it is a girl. And if you see a white flag, I pray you will all come home to me and let me see you again. But if you see a red flag, run as fast as you can and stop for nothing, and I will pray for you.

"And—I hope," she said, "that you would never be too hot in summer, nor too cold in winter, that the sun would not burn your faces, nor the wind tear at your clothes—that if I could not see you again, that you would not be lost from one another, that harm would not find you, and that death would not learn your names."

So her sons left with her blessing and fled into the woods. Each day, another of them would climb the highest tree and keep watch on the tower, but no flag appeared. On the eighteenth day, Elyas climbed the tree and saw a hand thrust a trembling flag through the topmost window of the castle.

"I see a flag," he shouted down to his brothers.

"The color," they called back. "Name the color of it, brother."

"I see red," he said. He knew it meant death, and he knew what death was, for his mother had told him. One of his elder brothers spat in the dirt by his feet. "Then we are to be turned out into the woods, and even die, for the sake of a girl?"

"The next girl I see," said another, "I'll kill it."

The hand and the flag vanished back inside the window, and Elyas came down the tree. "We'll move deeper into the woods," he said, "where none of us can be found, and none of us will be killed. We'll go so deep into the woods, we'll never have to see a girl, nor kill one neither." The rest of the brothers agreed with his plan, and set off in the direction where the oldest and tallest trees grew thickly together, where the only sunlight was filtered green and vanished early in the afternoon.

Here they built a house, a crudely hewn boys' house. The first winter they did not know to chink up the cracks with mud and straw and were bitterly cold. They did not know how to tell bad water from sweet and were sick for days. They did not know how to build a fire so that the smoke did not roil and blacken the ceiling, coating the whole house with soot. They did not know to follow deer to find salt for their meat. In short, they suffered. "All this for a girl," they said to one another in those days, and they swore again to kill the first girl they met. The next winter, they daubed the corners of their house to keep the wind out, and dug a well where clear water gushed up from the earth. And in this manner twelve years passed.

* * *

The king's wife had given birth to a king's daughter, and he named the girl himself. Her hair and her eyes were black, her voice was as clear as the waves breaking on the shore, and she was as lovely a king's daughter as anyone could wish. She ate from a little golden dish and drank from a little golden cup that he had made especially for her and placed right next to his own seat at the table. The king's wife again turned her plate out for the king's dogs, but now that she was not growing a daughter, nobody minded.

The king loved his daughter with all the ease and joy with which he had once loved his sons, and then some—he simply transferred the love he had felt before to her and added that which she merited through her own goodness to it. The king's wife loved the girl in spite of herself, and her love carried with it six times its weight in grief.

The girl knew she grieved her mother and tried to be less than she was so as to lighten her mother's burden. Once she chanced down a small corridor and saw six small rooms, with six small beds, and six small pairs of shoes arranged neatly in them. She asked her mother, "Whose are these rooms?"

And her mother told her the story of her birth, and took her up to the locked room, and showed her the six coffins with the goose-down pillows. Then the girl said, "Then I should never have been born."

"I love you, dear child," her mother said, which was not quite a contradiction.

The girl said, "My father the king loves me without

goodness. You love me without joy. I will go and find my brothers, and it may be we will be happy together." And so it was that the king lost all his children, and whether he got any more from this wife or any other woman, I cannot say.

The king's daughter, who should not have been born, took what belongings she could carry and went out into the forest, not knowing that her brothers hated her with all their hearts. The woods were green and gray, and filled with currents of cold air that carried no scent with them. She walked all of six days and into the seventh night, and her shoes were flimsy and full of stones. (But she had suffered as yet only a week; she could not yet match her brothers' twelve years.) When night was drawing to a close, she came to the little house. She went inside and found a young man, who looked frightened to see her. Being a king's daughter, she was used to the look of fear and was not surprised by it. "Where do you come from?" the young man asked her. "Who are you, and where are you going?"

"I am looking for my brothers, the king's sons," she said, "to apologize for being born."

"And you have found them," he said, for it was Elyas, her youngest brother, and they embraced each other with glad hearts.

"But, sister," Elyas said, pulling back from her, "my brothers hold a murderous grudge against all women and have sworn to put an end to any girl we meet."

"Oh," his sister said, as she had not expected that. "I had not expected that."

"They will not do it, I think," he said, "if they saw you, for then they would love you and wish to make you happy, as I do. You are lucky they left before dawn this morning to go hunting. But hide yourself under this washtub, and I will endeavor to set things right between us."

"Someday, I think," she said, her voice muffled under the tub, "I would like to meet someone I have not caused any pain."

"Be quiet," Elyas said. "I hear someone coming."

The door of the house swung open and in poured the brothers, now men, carrying with them all manner of game: red grouse tied together in fat clutches by the feet, bundled packs of snow cock, field-dressed barking deer and ibex. They threw their boots, crusted with game-blood and dirt, into the corner, and turned their catches over onto the table, so you could hardly see the wood beneath it.

"Little brother," one of them said, clapping Elyas on the shoulder, "this is a cold welcome! Where is the kettle? Where is the fire? What have you been doing with yourself while we were out hunting?"

Elyas asked, "Know you nothing?"

And his brother answered, "Nothing more than to find game, and to track it, and to hunt it."

"You have gone hunting, and I have stayed at home, but I know more than you," Elyas said. And his brothers smiled, for they loved a good riddle. One of them started a fire on the stove himself, not begrudging Elyas the making of it.

"We made a promise to each other once," Elyas said to

them, "that the first girl we saw, we would kill. Will you break that promise, if I ask you to do it?"

"Hungry men will break any promise!" his eldest brother shouted. "Tell us, Elyas, but for God's sake, feed us after the telling."

It had been many years since any of them had thought about the red flag or the promise they had made when they spat in the dirt and ceased to be king's sons.

"We'll harm no one you've put under your protection, little brother," one of them said.

"As for me, I am too weak from hunger to harm anything but dinner," said another. "Tell us, and have done, and pass me a crust of bread so that I may live to hear Elyas's news."

Then Elyas lifted up the washtub and out of it crawled their sister, with her black hair and her sorry eyes. "Here is the sister for whose sake we took to these woods," he said. "She is here to love us and be loved by us, if we will have her."

Her brothers stared in amazement, until at last the tallest among them, red-haired, brown-cheeked, and merry-eyed, clasped her by the waist and lifted her bodily above him. "What a plague you've been to us, little murderer," he said, but his voice was full of joy.

"What a mess you are," said another, smiling at her dark and curling hair. "Did you crawl through the woods on your hands and knees to find us, or are you just an unusually slovenly girl?"

"A waste, entirely," said a third, taking her in his arms and embracing her. "Shall we send her back to the king, brothers?"

"Surely," said another brother, leaning still against the doorway. "She'll be nothing but a burden to us."

"A terrible burden," the last said. "She shall have my bed, until I can build her one of her own. Though I've no doubt I'll catch my death of cold, sleeping on the floor."

"Put her by the fire," her oldest brother insisted, over the clamor. "She's weak as a calf, no doubt, and we'll have to coddle her exceedingly, though it cost us our own health."

And their sister beamed and wept through it all, though she could not bring herself to return their jokes.

"That's *me* you're hugging, idiots!" Elyas shouted. "Put me down."

* * *

After this, every day passed in swift and perfect happiness. Elyas and his sister stayed at home while the other five went hunting for roe deer and ptarmigan every morning, and between the two of them made quick work of housekeeping. They chopped wood for the fire, drew water for the cooking, and tended to the vegetable garden, so their table would not always depend on the luck of the hunters.

In the clearing by their little house grew six white lilies all in a row. One afternoon, wanting to bring some cheer into the house, the girl plucked them from their stems and gathered them into her basket. But in that same instant, her brothers were transformed into six bone-white swans, circled the sun overhead three times, and were gone. She clapped her hand to her mouth and wept bitterly, for now she had lost her brothers twice, and this time from her own fault more than the first. She scanned the sky for any sign of their return, until her eyes were red and weak, and she fell to the ground, exhausted from weeping, and fell asleep. And in her dream she saw her own mother, looking older and more grieved than she ever had before.

"Not-born," her mother said, "what have you done? Why could you not leave the lilies growing where they were? They were the only protection I could have afforded my sons, and now they have been transformed into birds forever. The only comfort I can take is that he who kills a swan will surely die himself."

"I am sorry," said the girl and wept.

"You were born sorry," her mother said. "I am sorry, too."

"Is there nothing I can do to help them, Mother?" she asked.

"No," she said. "There is one way, but it is so arduous, so solitary that I know you cannot accomplish it, you who cannot even leave a garden alone without tearing it up. You have murdered my sons' hopes twice, and my heart with them, and there will be no mending of it."

"Tell me what it is and I will do it," the girl said.

"You must suffer for them, as they have suffered for you," her mother said.

"I am not afraid to suffer," she said.

"Of course you are not afraid to suffer," said her mother. "The worst that has happened to you is a week's walk and a few stones in your shoes, and you do not know what there is to be afraid of."

"Nevertheless I am willing," said the girl. "I know I can do it. They toiled for twelve years on my account; I will do no less for them."

"You owe them each a year of silence," her mother told her. "You will never be able to do it. Six years—plus one for yourself—must pass before you can let a word or a laugh cross your lips. You may not sing, nor hum, nor whisper, not one word, or all your good work will be undone; not even a single minute before the seven years are up, for your brothers will surely die the moment you utter it."

"I will do it," the girl said.

"There is more," her mother said. "See you the stinging nettle I hold here in my hand? You would have to gather as many as you could, pulling them up firmly by the roots and withstanding the scalds and blisters they give you. You must grind them to bits under your feet and turn them into flax, silent all the while, then spin it and weave out of it six new shirts for your brothers to wear. You would have to find them and throw the shirts over them, before they could take their homely forms again."

"I will do it," the girl said.

"Remember their lives depend on your silence," her mother said. "You must not speak again from the moment you begin the work until it is finished. And I pray that you will not cause me more heartbreak than you have already. How God could send me so much pain in one so small, I cannot guess."

"I will do it," the girl said, "and as much as you and my brothers have suffered, I will see to it that you know twice as much joy hereafter."

"We shall see about that promise," her mother said. "You could have saved them with labor far less troublesome than this."

"What is that?" the girl asked.

"You could have not been born when I asked you to," her mother said, and was gone.

The girl awoke to find herself alone. There was a frilled patch of stinging nettles nearby, and slowly she began the sticky work of gathering them.

* * *

At sunset, her brothers returned to the house in a clot of beating wings. She looked up from her work and smiled to show her joy, but said nothing. There was blood on the floor. Her mother had not lied to her about the nature of suffering, and the girl found that one did not grow accustomed to pain with time, as one did with pleasure. Each new blister, each new pocket where her skin sloughed off and left a raw and oozing throb behind, each sting that worked its way into her bare feet, was as fresh and startling as the first. But while these pricks and gashes did not decrease with time,

she slowly became better able to bear them, or at the least
began to divide her day in terms of *less* and *more* pain. If
she could last until the sun cleared the garden wall, then she
could make it until noon, and by noon the day was half over.
Every night she was glad to be rid of another day, and in the
evening she had her brothers for company, if not compan-
ionship. At any rate, she had been born for suffering, and it
was time to get acquainted with it.

When three years had passed, she had completed three
and a half of her brothers' shirts. (She had spoiled the first
one with her clumsy work, and lost several days to weeping
and gnashing her teeth in silent fury.) She was working one
afternoon in solitude, her red hands flying about her, when
she heard the sound of a huntsman's horn. It had been a long
time since she had heard a sound made by anyone but herself, and it filled her with as much dread as if she had been
a roe deer. Quick as she could, she gathered up the nettles
in her apron and stuffed her brothers' shirts into her girdle.
She slipped out through the back door and found a tall tree,
which she climbed to the top, and seated herself among
the branches, and made herself as small as possible. There
she sat and spun while below her the winding of the hunting horn and the cries of the staghounds drifted ever closer.
She waited for the sounds to pass, and when she looked
down again, she saw a man looking back at her. He smiled.
She closed her eyes.

"What is your name, sweet child?" the man asked. She
said nothing. "You must not fear to speak to me—I am the

king of this country, and no harm will come to you as long as you are in it."

She closed her eyes even tighter and then opened them again. He had begun scaling the tree. She stuffed the rest of the nettles into her apron pocket before he could see them, and waited.

"How did you get up here?" he asked, casting down his hat to the men waiting below. He ascended to her seat, swung himself up beside her, and took her hand from her lap. "Never have I seen anyone so beautiful," he told her. Her hand felt dead where he pressed it. The man tore off his cloak and swept it around her shoulders. "You are too beautiful to remain here in these woods all alone," he declared, as if annexing her. "You will return with me, and I will see to it that you are dressed and honored as befits your station, because as surely as I am a king, you are a king's daughter."

Being beautiful had never prevented her from remaining in the woods alone before, but there was nothing she could do about it. Beauty was what gave him the right to talk to her as if they had been introduced, and take her hand, and make her wear his cloak, and take her from her tree and to his home. She could not help herself from crying, just a little bit, at the ridiculousness of it all. "Believe me, maiden," he told her, "the day will come when you will thank me as your deliverer, and if you are as obedient and good as you are beautiful, I will make you my queen." It was remarkable, the things he was willing to give her, although she had not asked for them. And if his men thought his behavior odd, they kept their thoughts to themselves.

The king seated her on his horse, just behind himself, and together they rode away. When next she opened her eyes, she saw in the sky a wedge of swans following them at a distance, and she smiled in her heart. One of the king's archers rose in his seat to take aim at them, but she grew so distressed, and her eyes so full of tears, that the king ordered him to leave off. She was so relieved, she fell asleep right there in the saddle.

She awoke to find herself riding through the gates of a great city, greater than the city her father had ruled, with great buildings, and golden cupolas, and fountains, and gardens with walls thirty ells high. The sun swept low and red over all of it.

They dismounted at the gates of a great marble building, the floors of which were covered in carpets richer and more sumptuous to the touch than her bruised feet could ever have hoped for. The walls too were hung with tapestries dazzling to the eye, but she did not see them for her tears. She could not understand how she was here, when she had never said yes to being brought anywhere. She could not remember speaking to him, much less agreeing. She was beginning to learn the danger of silence, and that someone who wishes to hear a yes will not go out of his way to listen for a no.

The king clapped his hands, and women rushed to attend her, to bathe her red, raw limbs in milk and wine and water, to dress her hair and massage sweet oils into her temples, to take from her the clothes she wore and dress her in courtly robes. At this she flew into a fright, and would not allow them to come near, until they left her apron and girdle folded on the floor before her. She swept them up in her arms and held them gently against her. The king laughed. "My silent tyrant," he said to his men. "She will have her own way. It is lucky she looks so pretty when she does." When she had finished dressing, the entire court bowed low in admiration of her beauty. "Do you see?" she heard the king exclaim to a tall man nearby, whom he was evidently proud of besting. "I will marry no one other."

"Majesty," said the man carefully, "she is beautiful, I cannot argue that—"

"If you did, I'd call you a fool and worse," the king said.

"But we know nothing of her. All she has done is cry. What kind of a king's wife will she be?"

"All women cry," the king said. "Another woman would not look so beautiful doing it, and trouble me all the more by adding speech to it." And before the man—blessed enemy that he was, she hoped he would compile a list of infamies against her—could say another word about it, the king called for music and dancing.

So it was that they were married, and as it turned out, getting married required as little speech from her as had leaving her home. Afterward the king led her through marble halls and fragrant gardens, though she neither spoke nor smiled but wondered how he could love such a silent, sad companion. The king opened the door of a little green chamber, on the floor of which he had placed her spinning things and a bundle of nettles. "Since nothing else seems to give you pleasure here," said the king, "in spite of all I do for you, here you may dream you are back in your old treehouse, and perhaps it will amuse you now, if all my kingdom does not."

She began to see how dangerous it was to be unhappy when he did not want her to be and smiled at him. He smiled back at her and ran his hands through her hair, and she stayed very still, so as not to upset him by shuddering. She wished now for the pain she had known in the woods, and would gladly have taken another seven years of blisters and stings and aching joints over these interminable caresses, but she had promised to suffer without distinction as to the cause.

"Open your eyes when I address you," the king told her, and pinched her sharply about the neck until she looked at him. "You return my generosity with such sullenness, such as befits a kitchen maid, rather than a king's daughter and a king's wife. Would you take all the joy out of my gift?"

She opened her eyes very wide and shook her head very hard.

"Good," he said. "Do not make me regret my generosity to you again."

* * *

After a year of this, the king's wife knew she was going to have a child. How she wished for her mother then! Here was a wholly new kind of pain. Surely she would be acquainted with every variety of suffering before this could end, but she could at last say she had earned the right to be born. She had completed four of the shirts now and kept them hidden in a small compartment underneath her bed, for the king had taken away the spinning room he had given her and snatched at her hands when he thought she had been working, to check for blisters.

"You have no right to ruin these hands," he told her, and tweaked her wrist until she sank to her knees. "Why do you wish to insult me, by marring what I love so dearly?" And then he would kiss her hands until he was on his knees beside her, and gather her into his arms, and whisper tender words to her. After that she did her work with gloves, although the wearing of them hindered her progress exceedingly.

One of her servingwomen, who was named Laila, was dearer to her than all the rest and knew her mind better than anyone. One evening, as the two of them walked arm in arm in the king's gardens, Laila asked her, "How long have you carried the king's child?"

The queen fanned out two fingers across her stomach.

"You will not be surprised, I think, to learn that you are not the first woman at court to do it," Laila said. "I can help you, if you wish it. Would you like to keep the king's child, and raise it, and be a mother to his son?"

And the queen shook her head. Behind her, a flock of swans landed noiselessly on the surface of one of the king's pools.

"Would you like to be rid of it now?"

The queen nodded. The swans drifted idly along the water.

That night Laila brought an evil-smelling cup to the queen's bedside and bade her drink it. The next day, Laila said to the king, "Your wife is unwell, and must not see anybody if you value her health." Three days later, the king had no child. It had only been an ordinary, common kind of suffering, and the queen was grateful for it.

The next year, after the completion of another shirt, the queen found herself in the same predicament as before. This time, the king's mother whispered to him that the woman he married was unlucky or worse, but he would not believe it.

"Have I not taught her to treat her hands as if they were my own? She has come to see that we are as one body, and that any crime she committed against herself would be a crime against my own person."

But the king could not make up his mind to dismiss these charges quite, and when the queen failed to keep his child a third time, he had her drawn up in front of the whole court and accused her. She was unable to speak in her own defense, and, unwilling that her servingwoman should suffer alongside her, she was condemned under the law.

It so happened that the day of her sentence was the last day of her seven years' silence. All but a single sleeve on the sixth shirt was done. As she was led away to the stake, she draped the shirts over her right arm. The king saw them and cried out at the sight: "Those accursed shirts! The witch was always secreting herself away, spinning and toiling at God knows what, and wishes to take her tokens with her—take them away! Strip her before she burns!"

She closed her eyes and heard the sound of wings. Before one of his men could reach her, the six swans landed in a circle at her feet, and her heart sang for joy. She threw a shirt over each of their heads, and the crowd drew back.

All her brothers stood before her, tall and clear-eyed and beautiful. One of them grabbed the king by the scruff of the neck and held him near the fire intended for her.

"Sister," he said, "is it your wish that this man should live? Only say the word, and we will spare him."

And she said nothing.

"You need not fear to speak now," Elyas told her, putting his arm around her. His shirt had lacked only one sleeve, and in place of the other arm, he retained a swan's wing, which he kept folded at his side. "The time is over, and you have suffered beautifully. There is no reason to hold your silence any longer."

The king struggled in her brother's grip. "Woman—woman—use the tongue in your head!" He hurled every invective imaginable at her—accusing her of spite, of obstinacy, of wretched ingratitude, of heartlessness, of a lack of womanly affection, of coldness—and she heard them all.

"Perhaps she would rather save her first words for something more deserving," Elyas said.

"Sister," her brother said, "I begin to weary of the tender

embraces of this kicking jackass, and I think I know how to address our situation. Say the word if you wish to spare him. Say nothing and I shall consign him to the flames and wish him the very best of luck with them."

She looked at her brother and was startled into smiling. She smiled at all her brothers then. She smiled at her husband, too. She said nothing. The flames grew very hot and very high.

FIVE

The Rabbit

THERE WAS ONCE A VELVETEEN RABBIT, AND IN the beginning he was really splendid. Later, he was something other than splendid, but this was the beginning, and splendid will do for a start. He was fat and sleek, as a good rabbit should be; his coat was skewbald with deep rust brown patches, he had real thread for whiskers, and the insides of his ears were slick with pink.

It was Christmas, and there were other presents in the boy's stocking, but the Rabbit was the best of them all. For at least two hours, the boy loved him, and then the family came to dinner in great clumps of aunts and uncles and cousins, and then there was a frantic unwrapping of parcels and papers. In the excitement of looking at all the new presents the Velveteen Rabbit was put aside, and he learned for the first time what it was to be ignored, and he did not forget it.

For a long time he lived in a cupboard with the other unnecessary toys, and no one thought very much about him. As he was made merely of velveteen, and his ears were of georgette, rather than real satin, some of the more expensive toys snubbed him, and he did not forget that either. The mechanical toys were very superior and looked down on everything that neither clacked, nor opened and shut on command, that was not a model of a plane or a boat or a car. Even the model train, which could run only on magnets along the track it was sold with, and could not be pushed along a table or the floor, never missed an opportunity to refer to his engineering in the most technical of terms. The Rabbit could not claim to be a model of anything, for he didn't know that real rabbits existed; he thought they were all stuffed with sawdust like himself. Sometimes he imagined what the other toys would look like with fistfuls of sawdust jammed into their open eyes and their painted mouths, down into their stomachs. Among them all, the Rabbit was made to feel very insignificant and commonplace, and the only one who was kind to him at all was the Skin Horse.

"Whose skin do you have?" the Rabbit had asked him, and the Skin Horse had shivered to hear the excitement in his voice. "Whose skin did you get?"

"Not like that," he explained. "Not skin like that." The Rabbit sat in silence, and the Skin Horse knew he had not liked the answer. The Skin Horse had lived longer in the nursery than any of the others, and he was so old that his coat was rubbed bald and most of the threads of his tail had been ripped out. He was wise, for he had seen a long succession of mechanical toys arrive and swagger and break their springs and pass away, and he knew they would never turn into anything else. The Rabbit would not be like the mechanical toys, and he would not let himself pass away. The Rabbit would not break for anything.

"What is Real?" asked the Rabbit one day, when they were lying side by side on the nursery floor. "Does it mean having things that buzz inside you and a stick-out handle?"

"Real isn't how you are made," said the Skin Horse—the Rabbit, who had quite liked the idea of having something buzzing inside of him, was rather disappointed at this—"but a thing that happens to you. When a child loves you for a long, long time—not just to play with—but really *loves* you, then you become Real."

"Does it hurt?" asked the Rabbit.

"Sometimes," said the Skin Horse, for he was always truthful. "When you are Real you don't mind being hurt quite so much." This was a relief to the Rabbit, who was more than a little let down by how dull being Real sounded.

"Can you hurt something else," asked the Rabbit, "when you become Real?"

"I don't know," said the Skin Horse, for he was always truthful.

"Can you take someone else's Real," he asked, "or are you stuck having to get it brand-new each time on your own?" The Skin Horse looked at the Rabbit then.

"What I mean is," the Rabbit said carefully, and his voice was a crawling black thing across the floor, "if something else was already Real, could you take it from them, and keep it for yourself?"

"No," the Skin Horse said. "You can't take Real from another toy." A truth, which was no small relief to the Skin Horse, who was no fool and could tell in what direction the conversation was tending. But the Rabbit had not yet finished with his questions.

"Can you take the Real out of a boy, then? Can you take his heart into your own self and leave him stuffed with sawdust on the nursery floor in your place?"

And the Skin Horse did not say anything to that.

"I suppose *you* are Real?" said the Rabbit, and the Skin Horse was afraid for the first time in a long while.

"Yes," he said quickly, closing his eyes. "From the boy's uncle. That was a great many years ago; but once you are Real, you can't become Unreal again. It lasts for always."

"I wonder if that's true," the Rabbit said.

"It is true," the Skin Horse said. "It's very true," and he kept his eyes closed.

"How did you make him?" the Rabbit, who was no longer lying down, asked with a terrible sort of eagerness. "How did you make him give it to you?"

But the Skin Horse did not move and did not talk again. The walls of the room were old and yellow and painted with late-afternoon shadows, and suddenly the Skin Horse felt he had been Real for too long.

After that the Skin Horse was seen no longer in the nursery, and the Rabbit's eyes gleamed a brighter black and his ears glowed a livelier pink.

* * *

In the nursery, there was a tiresome sort of person called the nanny. The nanny was difficult to anticipate; sometimes she took no notice of the things lying about, and sometimes, for no reason whatsoever, she swooped about the place like a windstorm and bundled all the toys away in cupboards. She called this tidying up, and everyone but the nanny hated it. The Rabbit especially hated it, and he did not forget the times he had been tidied. The Rabbit was not in the business of forgetting, especially once he decided that he had been cheated of something. After one such tidying, the Rabbit had been cheated of his place on the floor, and he would not forget it. The nanny was most assuredly not Real.

Sometimes the Rabbit thought it was entirely possible that nothing at all was Real, that Real had been a lie of the Skin Horse from the beginning. But if there *was* Real, the Rabbit would find it. If there was *not* Real, then the Rabbit would decide what would happen next.

One evening, when the boy was going to bed, he couldn't find the little white horsehair dog that always slept with him. The nanny was in a rush, so she simply looked about her, and seeing that the toy cupboard door stood open, she fetched the Rabbit out with an efficient hand.

"Here," she said, "take the old bunny—he'll do to sleep with." And she dragged the Rabbit out by one ear, and put him into the boy's arms, and the Rabbit felt the Realness of the boy's warm heartbeat and the boy's soft and fluttering throat, and he knew that the Skin Horse had not been lying.

That night, and for many nights after, the Velveteen Rabbit slept in the boy's bed. At first the Rabbit found it rather uncomfortable, for the boy hugged him very tight, and sometimes he rolled over on him, and sometimes he pushed him so far under the pillow that the Rabbit could scarcely breathe. The Rabbit found he missed the long, dark quiet of the nursery, when everything else in the house slept and was still. The boy did not sleep like everything else in the house. The boy slept in motion, and he snored, and rolled over, and grunted, and chapped his lips, and muttered in his sleep. The boy had jam on his bedclothes and shoved crackers in his flat and flabby mouth. But the Rabbit bore his discomfort graciously and waited for the boy to start loving him.

The boy insisted on talking to the Rabbit, spilling the secrets of his stupid and inane boy's heart, and he made ridiculous tunnels for the Rabbit under the bedclothes that he said were like the burrows that real rabbits lived in. Then the Rabbit knew that there were others like him and that the boy had kept him from them. And he did not forget that, and when the boy made him play his insipid games after the nanny had gone to bed, the Rabbit burned in shame and anger. But when the boy dropped off to sleep, the Rabbit would wriggle down under the boy's small hot chin and above his small hot heart and listen to his dreams. And then it was the Rabbit's turn to play.

On some mornings the boy would wake up dizzy and red-faced and cross and tangled in his bedclothes, and on some mornings the boy could not get out of bed at all. One morning, the boy woke up and was sick in the hallway. The Rabbit was his only comfort then, on mornings when his limbs were so sleep-heavy that he stumbled on the way to the kitchen and spilled his breakfast with a trembling hand, and he grew afraid of the body he lived in.

So time went on, and the little Rabbit was very happy.

Spring came, and there were long days out in the garden, for now the boy never went anywhere without his Rabbit. There were rides on the wheelbarrow, and picnics on the grass near the nursery door (the boy could not go past the flower border without becoming quite short of breath and complaining of dark stars behind his eyes). Once, when the boy slipped and fell down and had to be carried inside, the Rabbit was left out on the lawn until long after dusk, and the nanny had to come and look for him with the candle because the boy couldn't go to sleep unless he was there. The Rabbit was wet through and quite earthy from creeping along the burrows the boy had made for him in the flower-bed, and the nanny grumbled as she cleaned him off with a corner of her apron. She had not seen him when he was an inching, bunching thing streaming darkly through the tunnels under her feet, and the Rabbit rejoiced that he had not been seen until he wished to be.

"You must have your old bunny!" she said to the boy. "Fancy all that fuss for a toy!"

The boy sat up in bed and thrust out his shuddering hands. "You mustn't say that. He isn't a toy. He's *real*."

When the little Rabbit heard that, he was too happy to sleep. That night he grew fatter and sleeker and stronger, and into his boot-button eyes, that had long ago lost their polish, there came a look of happiness so bright that even the nanny noticed it the next morning when she picked him up, and she smiled to see it.

That day the boy was especially ill, and complained of a thick feeling in his lungs and dust in his eyes. The nanny was cross, for she was never ill, and there is nothing the healthy find more tiresome than the sick. "Is there anything else you need, love?" she said, bustling about the sickbed, but the Rabbit knew she meant "Why don't you get up and get better?"

"Why don't you get up and get better?" the Rabbit whispered to the boy that night. The next morning the boy woke with four teeth cracked open to the root.

* * *

Now it was summer, and the sun shone so hot that all the next month the servants found fox after fox lying along the edges of the grounds like gifts, mouths strewn open and flecked with white, quite dead from the heat.

Near the house there was a wood, and in the long summer evenings the boy liked to go there after tea to play, on the evenings that he could stand and keep both eyes open. He would march off brokenly, dragging a wagon with the Rabbit riding behind him. Some nights as the sun set, and his cracked lips bled, the boy would cry a long, noisy child's cry, and the Rabbit would endure it with perfect patience as the boy built him a nest and told him all his stupid, childish sorrows.

One evening, while the Rabbit was lying alone on the grass watching the light play over his own splendid paws, he saw two funny little creatures creep out of the tall brush near him. They were rabbits like himself, but differently made, as they seemed quite brand-new. Their joints didn't show in the least, and they changed shape queerly as they moved: one minute they were low to the ground and whispersome and the next thickly gathered together into a neat bundle of flesh. They slid and spilled about him, one quite the shadow of the other. The Rabbit stared as they crept close to him, looking for the key that wound them up and made them jump so. The rabbits stared back at him, twitching their noses all the while, until one of them finally asked, "Why don't you get up and run with us?"

"I don't feel like it," said the Rabbit, which was true.

"Don't you?" asked the other rabbit. "It's easy as anything." And he gave a great juddering lurch sideways and caught himself violently on his hind feet. "I don't believe you *can* do it," he said.

"I can," said the Rabbit. "I can run like anything and jump, too," and he meant it.

"*Can* you?" asked the laughing, lurching rabbit, and he shivered from side to side in a funny little hopping sort of dance. The grass behind him was pale, and the long, slim trees beyond paler still. The garden was a shuddering black thing, the winding path back to the house a ghastly river, white as termites. The Velveteen Rabbit could only sit madly in the middle of the pale path—he had no hind legs at all, only a single stiff-brushed cushion his head was sewn onto.

"I don't want to," he said again. But the slumping, slinking rabbits had very sharp eyes, and they peered at him and peered at him, and stretched out their necks wildly, and gaped at him as much as they pleased.

"He hasn't *got* any legs to run with," one of them said to his rabbit-shadow, and they each grinned at him with their mouths. "He hasn't got any legs to run with." The other creature bobbed his head up and down in gibbering agreement.

"I *have* got them," cried the little Rabbit wildly. "I have got them! I'm only sitting on them, and I don't care for you to see them!"

One rabbit danced closer and thrust his eyes up under the Velveteen Rabbit's nose, then shook his head and flattened his ears and jumped backward. "You don't smell right," he said. "You don't smell right at all, and you aren't anything that I know of, and you aren't real." The other twitched his nose in agreement.

Just then came the slow, slumping sound of the boy approaching, and with a fierce whirling of feet, the rabbits disappeared. For a long time the Velveteen Rabbit lay very still, looking at the grass and everything that moved over it and everything that moved under it. The sun trembled lower and lower in the sky until it tipped and spilled itself out over the grass. Presently the boy came limping back up the white path, and picked up the Rabbit and carried him home.

Months went by, and the Rabbit grew soft and tender like new skin from touch, and the boy loved him all the more for it. And the Rabbit loved him back. He loved the boy until his freckles faded and his head ached and his breath came in hard, sharp gulps like a dog's.

One day the boy caught a fever, and dark red patches bloomed high on his cheek, and he wept in his sleep, and his little body grew so hot it burned the Rabbit when the boy clutched him close. Strange people streamed in and out of the nursery, and a light began to burn all through the night, and through it all the little Velveteen Rabbit lay there, hidden under the bedclothes. The Rabbit found it a long and weary time, and worried that someone would spot him and take him away. But he knew how to be patient. He thought of the stupid Skin Horse, who had waited years to become Real. He thought very hard about what it would be like if the boy should get well again, and how they would go out in the garden and play splendid games in the raspberry thicket. All sorts of delightful things he planned, and while the boy lay half asleep he crept up close to the pillow and whispered them into his ear. The boy's skin grew white and thin as moth's wings. His joints seized up, thick and angry, and he cried out when his nanny moved his legs to change the sheets. The boy's teeth trembled and his eyes darkened and his brain had a fire inside of it. The boy *hurt*. And the Rabbit got Realer and Realer by the minute.

The boy no longer whispered his stupid secrets to the Rabbit, because his tongue had swollen up into every corner of his mouth. The boy scarcely moved. The boy gazed at the Rabbit and loved him, and the Rabbit loved him back very hard, until at last the boy stopped moving at all.

It was a bright, bold morning and the windows had been thrown wide open to let the breeze in. They had carried the boy out of the room, wrapped like a new toy. The little Rabbit lay tangled up among the bedclothes, with just his head peeping out, listening as they talked about arrangements and doctor's orders. The entire nursery was to be disinfected, and all the toys that the boy had ever played with were to be burned.

The Rabbit was very happy, to think of them all burned, although he was sorry to miss the disinfecting. He rather thought he would enjoy being disinfected, perhaps even as much as being Real.

Just then the nanny caught sight of him and popped him directly into the sack with old picture books and stiff-kneed toy soldiers and a lot of other rubbish, and carried them out to the end of the garden, where they were to be turned into a bonfire. The boy was not turned into a bonfire; the boy was wrapped up neatly and buried facedown in the dirt and, as he was no longer Real, the Rabbit promptly forgot him.

While the boy lay clench-fisted in the dirt, dreaming of whatever it is that not-Real things do, the little Rabbit lay among the old nursery clutter in the far corner of the garden, and he wriggled his head this way, and he wriggled his head that way, and bit by bit he was able to get his head through the opening and look out. Everything around him was going to be burned, all the boats, and the tin soldiers, and the little wheeled dogs on drawstrings, and the Rabbit only wished he could stay to see it.

But there were slick new pink muscles curling under his skin, and lungs unfolding at the end of his throat. He had a forest to visit, and two particular rabbits to see. He shook out his left leg, and that was Real. He shook out his right leg, and that was Real, too. He felt his warm heart beating inside his chest, as strong and as fast as a boy's.

SIX

The Merry Spinster

A RICH EXECUTIVE HAD THREE CHILDREN; SHE had other things besides, but for the purposes of this story, we will not concern ourselves with the rest of her inventory. Being a woman of sense and careful husbandry, she kept them well, always with an eye on the return of her investments. The two younger children were fine-looking; the eldest had weak eyes. When she was little she was called "the little Beauty" in jest, but she did not seem to notice the insult and answered to the name. Now she would answer to nothing else. She had no sense of when she was being praised or slighted. Instead, she read books, which did her no good whatever. She was twenty-eight and mostly useless.

Her two younger siblings had an instinctive sense of their own value and knew how to enjoy themselves. They went out of the house almost every day to school, to make modest purchases out of their discretionary accounts, to visit friends, to attend parties, concerts, civic engagements, and so forth, and they made themselves happy. They also read books, but only when they wished to and not because they were without alternatives; they answered to their given names. They did not mind Beauty's being mostly useless. They liked her anyway.

All at once, the executive lost most of her assets—her cash and cash equivalents, her securities and marketable investments—along with most of her inventory. She lost almost everything except for a vacation home she used as a rental property some distance from the city, and so turned out the tenants, who had not thoroughly reviewed their lease before signing, in an owner-move-in eviction.

Beauty was, perhaps surprisingly, more galled at the loss of the family fortune than her younger siblings, who had inarguably made more and better use of it. They, for their part, were concerned primarily with the happiness that money had bought them, and people who are determined to be happy can be happy anywhere. But Beauty had always found that the scarcer she made herself, the less life troubled her, so she began to get up at four in the morning to clean out the front rooms and get breakfast ready for the family. No one remarked on it, and so gradually she ceased to think of it as work and began to think of it as part of her nature. After she had done her work, she read, and continued to profit as little by it as she ever had. She still answered only to Beauty; in fact, she insisted upon it long after her siblings had found it necessary to continue making the same joke at her expense.

"You are *determined* to drudge," her brother, Sylvia, said one evening as she insisted on washing his coffee cup for him by hand. The family was all sitting in the same room they had eaten dinner in, and by this time, they had almost grown used to the practice. "We have a dishwasher," he went on, "and I know you know how to use it as well as anybody."

"Let her alone," Catherine said without looking up from the newspaper. "Beauty is determined not to thrive, and if you take the coffee cups from her, she might murder us all in our beds, just to have something to tidy up."

"I like to do it," Beauty said. "To clean the cups, I mean, not the bit about murdering you in your beds."

"What a tedious line that's becoming," their mother said. "I wish you would come up with something new to lie about, dearest. But you can take my coffee cup too, just the same, if it's important to you."

They continued more or less in the same vein for a year, when their mother, who had been cutting down on expenses by working remotely and hazarding her freelance earnings in speculation, learned that several of her recent investments had paid off handsomely and that the family could expect to reacquaint itself with money. Beauty's younger siblings nearly lost their minds with excitement as their mother prepared to visit her offices in the city once again.

"You *will* spit in the faces of all our old friends who turned their backs on us when we became poor, I hope, or else I will do something shocking and disgrace you," Sylvia said.

"We were never poor; we have a dishwasher," their mother remarked mildly. "And no one turned their backs on us. You've had five weekend guests in the last two months alone."

"I know," Sylvia said. "But I've always *wanted* to be able to spit in someone's face for turning their back on me for losing my fortune, and this may be as close as we're ever going to get."

"If it means that much to you, I can try to lose this money, too," their mother said.

"No," he said, after a moment's consideration, "although I appreciate your supporting my dreams. I'd rather you bring me back something extravagant and unnecessary and terribly expensive."

"All right."

"*Disgustingly* extravagant. *Vulgar.*"

"I'll do my best."

"Filthy."

"Sylvia," their mother said.

"*Filthy*," he said again firmly, and waggled his eyebrows until she smiled at him.

"I would be satisfied with a Packard," Catherine said, putting down the newspaper. "Or even a Citroën."

"Only one?" Sylvia joked, still waggling.

"Do not store up for yourself treasure on earth, Sylvia," Catherine said primly, "where moth and rust corrupt, and where thieves break in and steal. I'll take one now, and save the other for my birthday."

"What will you have, Bea?" their mother asked, having long ceased to humor her eldest child's perverse insistence on the name Beauty. "You should be rewarded for neither waggling your eyebrows like an imp nor for creasing the newspaper before I get the chance to read it, unlike certain of my other children."

"Where are these accursed offspring?" Sylvia said. "I'll teach them how to behave themselves."

"Sylvia, would you kindly decommission your eyebrows?" his mother said.

"Since you have the goodness to think of me," Beauty said, "be so kind as to bring me a rose." This was in fact a greater inconvenience disguised as a simple request; in trying not to think of herself, as she so often did, she burdened everybody.

* * *

Their mother left for the city. There was money to be set aside for taxes, and debts to be honored, and plenty of disputes with the other partners about what was to be done with the remainder, and after several discussions that she sorely wished could have come to blows, she returned home only a *little* richer than she had left. There were a few hours remaining in her journey when she found herself lost on a rarely trafficked road and out of gas. She had to leave the car parked on the shoulder and walk in search of a house with a telephone. It was raining madly, and the wind blew so fiercely that she could not keep her steps in a straight line. Night fell, and she heard the soft fall of footsteps behind her and felt the hot breath of something beside her.

Eventually, she saw a light through a line of trees and made for it, finding herself at the entrance to a great house. It was flooded from top to bottom with lights in every room, but the doorway was dark, with no lamp over it. The gate to the house opened easily enough, but no one came to the door at her knock. She found it unlocked and ventured inside, where she was met with a large hall, a well-established fire in the hearth, a fully dressed table, and not another living soul. She hallooed cheerfully and received no reply, then wandered a bit down the hall in case there was a phone she could use without disturbing anyone, but found nothing. She waited a considerable time, and still nobody came.

She had forgotten to be wary of hospitality with no host and drew near the fire to warm herself, planning just how she would explain herself should the owner of the house find her thus. *For*, she thought, *I can hardly be expected to go back to the car at this hour*, and decided she would be very charming when she *was* found, to make up for her bad manners.

Since she had already begun to be rude, she thought to herself sometime later, by entering the house and sitting by the fire uninvited, there was no great harm in eating from the dinner laid out on the table. She took a piece of chicken and ate it, and only afterward did she wonder at her own presumption. Then she thought she might like to have a glass of wine, and did not wonder at herself any longer; nothing about her situation seemed especially unusual after that. After a few more glasses, it occurred to her that she might like to explore the grounds. So, taking both the bottle and her courage with her, she went out of the hall, crossed through several grand rooms, all beautifully appointed, until she came to an enclosed courtyard and a garden within it. Passing under a cluster of hothouse roses, she was reminded of Beauty's request and twisted off a branch that held several blossoms; immediately she heard an unwelcome noise behind her and turned.

"How particularly uncivil," said the man—*was* it a man?—to her. "I have saved you from an exceedingly uncomfortable and dangerous night by the side of the road by opening my home to you, and not only have you drunk enough wine for several guests, but I find you stealing my property. I ought to shoot you for your trespass."

She had enough of a flair for the dramatic that she could not help but drop the bottle. "There's no excuse for it," she said.

"Be careful that you don't embarrass yourself."

"Would it insult you very much if I tried to apologize?"

"I am afraid that it would."

"Would an explanation prove equally offensive?"

"It would depend on the explanation, madam."

Now she felt herself on slightly surer footing, since he seemed inclined to allow her to be charming at him. She opened her eyes quite wide and tilted her head in as becoming a manner as she dared, remembering that she was past forty. "It was for my daughter," she said, hoping to sound more like an eccentric rich woman than a desperate and moderately impoverished one. "She had a particular inclination for a rose."

"You are holding several roses," he said.

"You are looking at an indulgent mother," she said, "my good man."

"I am neither of those things," the man-who-was-not-a-man replied, "but you might call me Mr. Beale, and don't bother with any more cute speeches. But you say you have a daughter who is fond of roses, and you look like a woman who is amenable to conducting a bit of business. I will overlook the trespass and I will *not* shoot you"—her knees relaxed considerably at that, much to her embarrassment— "on the condition that she should come here willingly in your place and stay here with me."

"How awful," she said without thinking.

"Yes," he said. "Let's not speak any further about it, but go about your business. You'll find a bedroom down the hall to your right that will suit you, and in the morning you'll find a car at the front of the driveway ready to take you home."

She began to wish she had not dropped the bottle.

"The Packard," he added before he disappeared. "I didn't have time to locate a Citroën. You have a red wine stain around your mouth."

She was reluctant to offer any of her children, even Beauty, to something so monstrous and polite but she was even more reluctant to be shot, and mothers have given their children to monsters before. The thought caused her great grief, but it was not great enough for her to do anything else; in the morning, feeling not a little guilty from her long and untroubled sleep, she drove the Packard home without looking behind her. It handled like a dream.

Once home, the children crowded around her, and she immediately burst into tears.

"Stop crying, Mother. I don't *mind* that it's only the 'twenty-seven model," Catherine said. "A Packard's a Packard."

"Here are your roses," she told Beauty as she wiped her nose. "I'm afraid they cost a bit more than I thought they would." Then she told them about what happened after her car broke down, about the great house flooded with light, and the dinner table with no guests, and what the owner of the house had said to her when he found her in his garden.

"But that's ridiculous," Sylvia said. "For starters, Beauty isn't worth a single flower, let alone a whole branch's worth.

I'll go live with the Beast, and send Beauty a postcard, if I ever get out of bed."

"He might outrage your virtue," Catherine said.

"I should *hope* so," Sylvia said.

"Better not risk the youngest, and the fairest hope of our family purity besides; I'll go, and I won't send anyone a postcard."

"I don't mind," Beauty said. "If I've been sent for, then I'll go."

"You idiot," Sylvia said, but there was no real rancor in his voice. "Can't you tell when you're being protected?"

"Not especially," Beauty said, which was true.

Their mother, who really loved Beauty very much despite herself, burst into tears again.

* * *

"What could he *want* with her?" Catherine whispered from her bed after she had turned out the lights.

"You don't have to whisper," Sylvia said. "It's not a secret, and Beauty has her own room. She's probably asleep already. I'll bet she sleeps the whole night through, even."

"It just feels like something one ought to whisper about," Catherine whispered.

"Do I have to whisper, too?"

"Not if you don't want to."

"Well, he's demanding, and solitary, and wealthy as the Devil, if he can afford to set a table for an imaginary dinner party every night just in case a disoriented motorist stumbles in off the street. And Beauty is ugly and doesn't know how to talk to anyone. So I can only assume it's some sort of elaborate sexual parlor game."

"Be serious, Sylvia."

"Uglier women than Beauty have married, you know."

"Sylvia."

"Not that he's strictly asked her to marry him. But as good as."

"*Sylvia.*"

"Well, they have. And she is. So it's true."

"If it's true, then it doesn't need to be said, does it?"

* * *

Some time passed, and nothing happened, and Beauty's mother, who did not enjoy feeling afraid, began to think that perhaps nothing would come of it after all.

Then: "A man in a mustache is at the door to see Beauty," Sylvia said one afternoon. "He looks as though he were going to speak German at me."

"I don't speak any German," the man said, bristling.

"Well, you look as if you do," Sylvia said, "and that's hardly my fault, is it? Not that it's yours either," he added kindly.

"What man—mustachioed or clean-shaven—would come all the way to our front door just to see one of my children, who are barely fit for public consumption?" their mother shouted from her study. "Send him back, wherever he came from."

"I am here on behalf of Mr. Beale," the man said, although no one had addressed him.

"He's here for Beauty's *assignation*," Sylvia said, loud enough for everyone to hear. "Where shall I put him, Mother?" But his mother did not answer.

"I'd send you to the boathouse to meet her," Sylvia said solemnly to the man at the door, "only we don't have a boathouse any longer."

After Sylvia had been made to apologize—"You don't *really* look like you speak German," he said, "and you may come inside to kidnap my sister, and that's as much politeness as you're going to get out of me"—the man was fixed up with a cup of coffee, which he did not drink, at the kitchen table with the family gathered around him. The man explained what was going to happen to Beauty. He had a contract in his briefcase.

"Is your man Mr. Beale going to do something *shocking* to her?" Sylvia asked hopefully.

"No," the man said. Sylvia kicked the legs of the table.

"I don't know that I want to belong to anyone," Beauty said. "I agreed to go, but this is something else entirely."

"Look at it this way," Catherine said. "Everyone belongs to someone. You're not allowed to belong to yourself. We haven't the money anymore and you never had the sense, and there's no point in pretending otherwise. You can't wait out your turn. You'll have to play, and the longer you put it off, the worse your position gets."

Beauty didn't answer.

"Here's another way to look at it, then," Catherine said. "Right now you belong to everyone in the family, and you can see what a mess that's turned out to be. At least this way you'll only belong to one person. That's something, you know. It's not much, but it is something."

"All right," Beauty said. "I'll go. But I won't have a good time."

"No one's asking you to," Catherine said. "You're the one who insisted on going in the first place, so you're free to be as miserable as you wish to be once you get there."

"Can I bring my books with me?" Beauty asked, and no one objected, which was as good as a yes.

"Call when you can," her mother said, bursting into tears again, even though it had already been agreed that she would be allowed to accompany Beauty to the house and see that she was safely installed there.

"I've packed all your socks, and the shirts that don't make you look washed-out," Catherine said. "The rest I'm going to burn. You have terrible taste in shirts, Beauty." Catherine kissed first Beauty, then their mother, and shoved the suitcase hastily into the car with them.

"Come back anytime you like, Mr. Beale's man," Sylvia shouted as they drove away. "You're welcome to outrage *my* virtue next, but I can't promise I'll have any left, if you dawdle about it."

The house was very quiet after that.

* * *

They took the main road to Mr. Beale's house, and toward evening they saw it lit up like a furnace against the horizon. The house threw off such heat from the enormous fires stoked in each room that it melted all the snow in a great ring around it.

Mr. Beale's man parked the car in the garage, and Beauty and her mother went back into the great hall, where the table was once again set lavishly, as if for an enormous celebration. Her mother had at first no heart to eat, but Beauty set about serving her as if they were at home, and she ended up doing modest justice to a chop and some clear soup. There was the heavy fall of footsteps just outside and the breath of something in the doorway, and then a Beast was with them. Beauty did not turn. Her mother dropped her soupspoon.

"Has she come willingly to me?" the Beast, who was Mr. Beale, asked. "Have you come of your own accord, girl?"

"I think so," she said, which was good enough for everyone involved.

Mr. Beale said, "Good." He turned to her mother. "Woman, go home, and never think of coming here again while I am living. You might have dessert first, before you go."

Then Mr. Beale turned, and then there was the heavy breath of something in the doorway, and then there was the heavy fall of footsteps on the stairs, and then there was nothing.

"I think," Beauty's mother said, shaking a little, "that you had better go home after all, and let me stay here, even if he does want to shoot me."

Beauty said nothing, and her mother hated herself a little for not meaning a word of what she had offered. "I am sorry," she said. She meant *that* sincerely, at least.

"I'll be fine," Beauty said.

Her mother could not help but cry again as she left, but who can cry or even feel sorry forever? Who will not eventually clear themselves of guilt, if they live long enough? She was not so sorry that she could not find pleasure in being free of that house, and she still had two other children. So she went home.

After her mother left, Beauty picked up one of her books and pointed her face at it and turned the pages— almost as if she were reading it. She felt sick and hot from the nearness of the fire, but decided it did not matter, as the Beast (for he was *more* than simply not-quite-a-man, he was *quite* a Beast) was likely to shoot her, or devour her whole, before much longer. Although not all Beasts eat you up in a single night.

However, she thought she might as well walk around the house until she was eaten, or shot, as she could not help admiring it. It was—unusually for such an obviously expensive home—designed with comfort in mind. She was perhaps less surprised than she ought to have been to see a door with the words "Beauty's Library" written over it. She opened the door and found a room of grand proportions, with hundreds of shelves built right into the walls and wrapping all the way around, each one filled with books. There was a pianoforte too, with dozens of music books, but what caught

Beauty's attention was that the books she had brought herself were already shelved with the others, although she had not put them there.

If Sylvia had been there, he might have said: "If Mr. Beale were going to kill me, he would never have gone to such trouble building me a library first, unless he enjoyed inciting confusion as much as he enjoyed killing, in which case he would have." But Sylvia was not there, and Beauty did not think either of those things. She took a book at random from one of the shelves and read these words:

> *The library is yours.*
> *The books are mine.*
> *Your eyes are your own.*
> *What you read is up to me.*

Beauty put the book back onto the shelf and left the room. She found her bedroom (the words "Beauty's Bedroom" were over the door) and sat on her bed. She did not leave her room again until late the next day. In the great hall she found dinner ready, and while she was eating, heard an excellent concert of music, but could not see the players who produced it. She had the strange certainty that she was to be often left alone but never left in private. Her hands shook so that she could not quite bring the fork to her lips without spilling anything, so she set it down. Then she laughed without meaning to.

Later, when she was seated there again for supper, she

heard the sound of Mr. Beale on the stairs, and then he was in the chair beside her. "Beauty," he said, "will you let me watch you eat?"

"It is your house," she answered.

"Not precisely," he said, "not precisely. My house it may be, but you are the mistress here—I have made it so, so it's legitimate—and you need only to tell me to leave, if you find me troublesome, and I will leave you."

"If I am mistress here"—she did not look at him—"why do I have a library full of books I cannot read?"

"Why, Beauty," Mr. Beale said in amazement, tilting her chin so that she had to look at him, "that is simply a matter of the division of labor. You are the mistress of the *house*"—he arranged his mouth in a little smile—"and I am the master of everything that is in it." He dropped her chin and let his hand rest in her lap. "How ugly do you think I am?"

Beauty said nothing.

"Come, you are mistress of your own voice; speak," said Mr. Beale.

Beauty opened her mouth.

"But first remember I am the master of all the words spoken in this house," he said, pressing her hands lightly. "Remember that."

"I think nothing of the kind," she said.

"You may go to bed," he told her, smiling. "I will finish your dinner for you."

Beauty rose to leave. "Please endeavor to amuse yourself in your house," Mr. Beale said after her, "for it belongs to you, and always will, and I should be very uneasy if you were not happy."

Beauty had nothing to say to that. She went to her bed and lay herself down in it.

* * *

Beauty sat among the books all the next afternoon, but she did not open the books. She did not open the curtains. She let the hours pass over her. That night at dinner, Mr. Beale was especially kind. He inspected every oyster before he would allow one on her plate, and she ate them all. Afterward, he asked her: "Beauty, will you be my wife?"

She was some time before she answered, for she did not yet know which words were not allowed in her house. At last, however, she said, "No, thank you."

Immediately he got up and smothered the fire that had been burning in the hearth. "Good night, Beauty," he said, as cheerful as ever. "Sleep well."

That night, long after Beauty went to bed, she heard the careful press of feet just outside her door. When she woke in the morning, every fireplace in the house was dark, and the carpets and the drapes were full of smoke. When she went to the library, she saw the title on every one of her books had been burned away to ash.

The next night at dinner, Mr. Beale did not enter the room but stood in the doorway. "Beauty," he said gently, "these chairs are for my wife. Are you my wife?"

"No, Mr. Beale," she said.

"Then what right have you to sit on my wife's chair?"

"None, Mr. Beale," she said.

"Where do you think you should sit, Beauty? Remember I want only for you to feel as if you are at home here."

Beauty took her plate and sat on the floor.

* * *

Beauty spent three months in Mr. Beale's house. Every evening Mr. Beale paid her a visit and watched her eat and talked to her. Every night before she went to bed he would ask her to be his wife. One night she said to him, "Perhaps you should stop asking me this."

"You think I should?"

"I think it might make you—*happier*—to not have to hear the same answer, at least for a while. I will stay here with you, and I do like you, and I am grateful to you for all you have given me, but I cannot marry you. I cannot marry anyone."

"I must grieve, then," said Mr. Beale. "What a great misfortune is mine, to love you as I do without hope."

"To be fair," she said, "you did not make our being married a part of the original terms."

"I did not," Mr. Beale said lightly. "More fool I."

"Perhaps you would not like being married to me," Beauty said. "I do not know how to talk to people, and I have terrible taste in shirts."

"If you will not marry me," Mr. Beale said, "perhaps I will die of grief."

Beauty's expression did not change. "I'm so unused to compliments. I'm afraid that I take them quite seriously."

"If you do not marry me," Mr. Beale went on, "it might kill me quite dead, and then this house would have no master at all, and you would belong to no one, and no one would belong to you. For, Beauty, I belong to you quite already. Does this mean nothing to you?"

When Beauty did not answer, he rose and pressed a thumb against her forehead. "Good night, Beauty."

That night, Beauty dragged the blankets off her bed and slept on the floor underneath it. Mr. Beale paced the halls all night, and he called after her, but he could not find her.

"Your poor Beast shall die of grief," he said. "I would not like to make a murderer out of you, dear Beauty."

Beauty did not come out from under the bed.

"Yet I would happily die," he said, "rather than cause you a moment's unease. Is it your wish that I should die, Beauty? Tell me if you wish it. Tell me if you would like me to die and I will do it, Beauty, Beauty, Beauty.

"Or I can beg for my life," he said. "I can beg, Beauty." She pressed her hands against her ears and waited. Then his footsteps fell away and were swallowed up by the house's great silence.

After three days had passed, Beauty came out of her room. Somewhere in the house lay Mr. Beale, and he was either quite dead or keeping himself extremely still. She went first into the kitchen and drank directly from the tap for two and one-half minutes. Then she went looking for

Mr. Beale. She found him lying facedown by the front door. She prodded him with her foot, but he did not move.

Beauty went into the back parlor and telephoned her mother. "Something's wrong with Mr. Beale, Mamma," she said. Then, a bit louder: "I think something's wrong with Mr. Beale. You had better come right away." Then Beauty went into the library and sat down. She did not touch the books, for they still did not belong to her, no matter how dead Mr. Beale may have been; she had never been his wife. She began to write Sylvia a postcard.

SEVEN

The Wedding Party

THEY HAD LEFT THE WINDOW OPEN THE NIGHT before, and the late morning sunlight insinuated itself vaguely throughout the room, encouraging the growth of the fine and robust hangover that had established itself underneath David's eyelids sometime between three and four, when he and Alison had finally gone to bed.

"Witching hour," he had giggled into his pillow. "I'll take my wife to bed in the witching hour; do you think that's much of an omen for married life?"

"Not your wife yet," she had said, "and not the witching hour either. It's the devil's hour, this hour, and I've got thirty—make that thirty-one—hours before you get to turn me into a wife."

"Thought it was witches," he said, trying to frown thoughtfully and failing, "for the witching hour. When they"—he waved his hand in a vague circle—"witch about. As they do. Render babies for broom grease, and break clocks, and dance in the nude for the purpose of blighting crops." He propped himself up on an elbow. "And you *are* my wife, or as good as, anyhow, so don't go trying to duck out now on a technicality. What am I supposed to do with all these place settings and linens if I haven't got a wife that goes with them?"

Alison said nothing but dropped a palm on his face and groped around until she found his nose with her fingers and gave it an affectionate tweak. He made to grab her hand, but his limbs had turned to water at some point between the evening's several toasts, and they merely chased themselves around, loose and pliant, before falling back at his sides.

"I expect it's hard for witches," he went on, "now that most people work in shops and factories, and haven't any crops to ruin. They must be terribly sad, those witches, to have to go from blighting wheat fields to blighting houseplants."

"The devil's hour," Alison repeated, "has nothing to do with witches whatever. Witches don't enter into the thing at all. Hour of the crucifixion darkness, on account of how Christ died in the afternoon. The inverse, I mean. Christ died at three in the day, so the devil's hour comes at three in the night."

There was a brief silence, and the room wobbled dementedly until David squeezed his eyes shut and forced everything back into its proper corner. "Terribly sad," David said solemnly. "Terribly sad, all those poor benighted witches dancing about in the nude without even the slightest crop to ruin.

"If you should like to dance in the nude and blight crops after we are married," he added, "I would be willing to sacrifice a Ficus or an orchid for your happiness."

"Thou shalt not be afraid of the terror by night," Alison mumbled into the arm thrown across her face. "Nor for the arrow that flieth by day, nor for the pestilence that walketh in darkness, nor for the destruction that wasteth at noonday; a thousand shall fall at thy side, and ten thousand at thy right hand, but it shall not come nigh thee." Then: "You're going to have a terrible head in the morning."

"I thought Harold looked awfully unwell tonight," he said. "Didn't you think he looked bad? Everyone said he was looking worse than a month ago." He rolled his head in Alison's direction and saw her eyes were already shut tight.

"The Ninety-First Psalm, verses five through—five through something," she said. "Harold has always looked terrible." Then she fell violently asleep.

Alison's prophecy had not gone amiss; David's hangover

that morning was the sort that pushed stout men of business out of windows. He might have considered it too, but the window was all the way on the other side of the room from the bed, and his legs appeared to have been coated with some sort of fast-setting metal alloy in the night. *Did* alloys set, he wondered, then decided it didn't matter.

"I'm going to lead a finer and nobler life," David said. He paused, noting that his tongue seemed to have tripled in weight over the night; it now appeared to terminate somewhere down in the neighborhood of his knees. "Full of integrity, and sobriety, and lemon water." His kidneys pulsed like two fat, poisoned hearts beating in his sides.

"*Are* you?" Alison asked. She did not move. "Am I going to be dragged into this new nobility, or can I merely sit back and observe?"

"I was not speaking to you, woman," David said. "I was addressing my hangover, who is a vigorous young squire of twenty-seven, with a wife and several children besides. Currently he is playing a game of horseshoes with ship anchors just underneath my skin, and cannot be disturbed. Also, you are lying down, and your eyes are closed, which would make observing anything a challenge, even for you."

"Are we going to be introduced?" Alison asked.

"I don't think I would like you two to meet," he said, organizing himself into a sitting position against the headboard.

"But look," she said, "I think he recognizes me. It would be rude of you not to acknowledge the acquaintance."

"He is not of the best society," David said. "You do not move in the same circles; you must be mistaken."

"I might open my eyes if you introduced us," she said, butting her head against his shoulder. "Then again, I may never open them again, and become a permanent addition to this bedroom. You won't need me for the wedding break-fast; I'll send a traitorous serving girl in a thick white veil, just like the true bride did in the fairy story, and you can marry her."

David shook his head lightly, so as not to disturb the team of blacksmiths at work therein. "That wouldn't work. I should know you."

"Ah," Alison said, "you would not know if I sent her with my mother's gold ring, my father's chain, and my own nut-brown hair, and her face covered besides."

"There's a horse in that one, I think," David said.

"Falada. He's dead; he's no good to you."

"A dead horse is *extremely* useful to a bridegroom who knows what he's about," he chided. "Aren't you supposed to be an educated woman?"

"No. Purely decorative. I read a story once; it was ter-rible and my head ached for days. It's still aching now, and if you try to make me remember another detail, I shall lose all my beauty, and you'll have no one to marry you tomor-row but a grim and loathly lady, who keeps house with ter-mites and rat poison."

"The horse—" David said, or tried to.

"Falada. It's 'The Goose Girl' story you're thinking of;

that's the only version of the false bride tale that's got a horse in it, and the horse is named Falada."

"Falada, then. Stop interrupting," he said, in a tone that suggested he knew she would not. "He was a gift from your mother, and no disguise can fool him, not even after the traitorous serving girl steals your clothes and your name and passes herself off as the true bride while you are reduced to tending a flock of sheep—"

"Geese."

"Geese, then, and when the serving girl passes under the church gate, he'll—"

"Why would a dead horse be waiting for a bridal party at the church gate?"

"A kind slaughterer nailed his head to the top of the arch. *Because*," he said before she could speak again, "because the true bride begged him to, and he could not refuse her request. And when the serving girl passes under the church gate, Falada would call out, 'Alas, if your poor mother only knew, her loving heart would break in two,' and that's how I'd know. Bridegrooms always know their true brides, through the strategic use of horse heads and love tokens."

Alison shook her head. "You wouldn't know if I sent her," she said. "You wouldn't know if the horse went to the tannery instead of the church gate, and lost his tongue altogether."

David turned his head and looked at her then. "I suppose I wouldn't," he said. Her dark hair was fanned out over her pillow, snapping with gold in the morning light, and she smiled up at him.

"Maybe you're not the bridegroom at all," she said in a singsong little voice. "Maybe you're the goose boy, chasing his hat—*Blow, wind, blow, take Conrad's hat and make him chase it, until I have braided my hair, and tied it up again. A goose boy, tumbling after nothing, while I tie up my hair.*"

"*Alison,*" he said.

"Maybe you're the horse's head, nailed over the gate, telling everyone who passes below you how much their mothers' hearts are breaking. Nailed, and dead, and staring." Her voice rose in a steady drone, monotonous and tuneful and lovely. "Oh, Falada, Falada, thou art dead! All the joy in life has fled! Falada, Falada—"

He was dimly aware, when he came back to himself, that the voice repeating her name was his, and that Alison was trying to wrench her arms back from him. He dropped his hands to his sides, and they broke apart.

"If you've left a mark," Alison said lightly, studying her wrists as she turned her hands over, "that would be extremely tiresome. You know I'm not wearing gloves with my suit tomorrow." Alison was enormously proud of her hands. So, for that matter, was David. She had a habit of looking pityingly at the ring he had bought her with such indulgence that it never failed to make David want to snatch it off her fingers and make her beg for it back.

"I'll buy you gloves this afternoon," he said.

"I don't *want* to wear gloves," she said. "Gloves look

priggish on a bride." Then: "It would be easier if you were able to refrain from *grabbing* me, darling. Cheaper than buying me a pair of gloves every time you do."

"I don't intend to make it a habit," David said stupidly. "Only—that wasn't like you, just then. I didn't like it."

"I'm sorry for frightening you, David," she recited, and her voice suggested more than a little of the schoolroom. She grabbed both of his wrists in a light echo of where his hands had been on her and twisted them gently. "Today I will clean my plate, and say, 'How do you *do*' when your mother greets me instead of spitting and baring my teeth, and protect you from officious bridesmaids"—she was laughing now, a real laugh, and David could not help but grin back at her—"and go to bed at a reasonable hour, and tomorrow morning I will marry you, and never give you cause to be frightened or make you feel you must threaten to buy me gloves ever again, I do solemnly swear."

She kissed him on both temples, her lips blessedly cool. "And I'll bring you aspirin for your hangover, and be a sober, faithful helpmeet for your new fine and noble life." Then she kicked her feet free of the blankets, dropped her legs over the side of the bed, and got up. He could hear her singing from the next room as she dressed her hair.

"It was intill a pleasant time,
Upon a summer's day,
The noble Earl of Mar's daughter
Went forth to sport and play.

As thus she did amuse herself,
Below a green oak tree,
There she espied a sprightly dove,
Set on a tower so hie.

'O Coo-my-dove, my love so true,
If you'll come down to me,
You'll have a cage of good red gold,
Instead of simple tree:

I'll put gold hinges round your cage,
And silver roun the walls;
I'll see you shine as fair a bird
As any of them a'.'

But she had not these words well spoke,
Nor yet these words well said,
'Til Coo-my-dove flew from the tower
And lighted on her head."

Her head appeared around the doorway. "David," she said, looking at him intently, "don't wear your blue suit today. Tess hated you in blue last night. She said you looked like a traffic policeman."

* * *

By midafternoon, offset with aspirin and a tentative attempt at lunch, David's hangover had receded into a general, unobtrusive air of listlessness. Even his headache felt dreamy and hardly worth noticing, and he allowed himself to be drawn from the street into the reception hall (which was something less than a hotel and something more than a teahouse) with dazed good grace. Then they sat and waited for Tess.

The kitchen was closed until five, the waitress had said, but she would bring them coffee and sandwiches, if they wanted. "I can't imagine wanting either," Alison said, "but you might bring me a champagne cocktail, if you're willing to part with one, or else nothing."

David smiled by way of apology. "Two champagne cocktails," he said, "or else two of nothing." The waitress nodded and disappeared through the back door, either to find their drinks or because she couldn't stand the sight of them another minute.

"I just want you to know," Alison said, "that it doesn't matter to me, if you like Tess."

"I do like Tess," David protested, aware it was impossible to sound sincere while saying so—and rather resenting her for opening a conversation with both a denial and an assertion of fact. He disliked fighting on two fronts. "I *should* like Tess. I do like Tess. And Tess should like me. *You* like me."

"I don't think that's strictly necessary." Alison had a habit of replying only to a selected portion of David's conversation, that which she considered worth discussing, and blandly ignoring the rest. It was a terrifically effective strategy; he had never been able to drag her back to a point once she had decided to abandon it.

"*Does* Tess like me?" David asked.

"I haven't the faintest idea," Alison said. "She hasn't done anything to suggest she doesn't, has she?"

"No, not exactly, only—she looks at one as though she disapproves of how one parts one's hair, or spells one's name, somehow."

"There's only the one way to spell David."

"All right, but I still got the distinct impression last night that she was disappointed by the sight of me."

"Perhaps she was," she said lightly. "I'll let you know, if she tells me, and do my best to provide further evaluation so you might make improvements."

"*Dar*ling," he said.

"*Dar*ling," she said, bowing her head.

"What I can't understand is why you put up with it."

"I don't need her to approve of you," she said. "*I* approve of you."

"I don't mean what she thinks of me, or doesn't. I mean all of it."

"Tess has always been singular. She has what she calls her *insistments*. She drew a single room every year at school but ended up making sure I bunked with her anyhow. It's better to let her get her own way. She doesn't require anyone else to do anything about it, so it's no trouble. I don't mind it."

The front door opened halfway, and a man looked in, scanning the room, then just as suddenly withdrew his head and shoulders back into the street.

"That's another thing," David said, striking his leg. "These demands, these whims she's got. You come home from those sudden trips of hers looking half-starved and half-mad, without a word about where you've been or how you got there. They're absurd. I can't imagine how you've put up with it so long, or why."

"Well, Tess is absurd. Lots of people are absurd. I don't see why it should bother you. We don't have to see her often after we're married, if that's what worries you."

"But that you should have to put up with it," he said. "When I think of all you've— Why hasn't she offered to help, even once?"

"David." She smiled, but there was a grimace behind it.

"She's simply rolling in it, and here you've been, living in what's more or less a garret because she thinks it's funny—"

"—sewing artificial flowers by candlelight, thumbs bleeding, throwing the family Bible and the last of my stockings into the fire to keep from freezing to death—"

"Laugh if you like, but for all that she's your oldest and dearest friend, she was certainly unconcerned enough about your going to work when she could have easily covered your share of the rent with what she spends on lunch."

"Oh, lots of girls work in shops. And I don't live with Tess because she has money. I live with Tess because we both particularly like it—and it hasn't stopped me from sleeping in your bed when I feel like it. Soon I'll be living with you, because you and I would both particularly like it, and you can pay as much of the rent as you want. Something in the neighborhood of all of it would satisfy me, I think." She put her arms around him and tugged him to her, and he let his head drop against her shoulder. "Don't let's quarrel over it, *dar*ling."

"*Dar*ling," he said, only a little muffled from speaking directly into her lapel.

"I've never wanted money from Tess," she said, "and I wouldn't have liked it if she had tried to give me any." The door opened again, and she braced David back up in his own chair and smoothed her skirt. "That's her now, and here you are with the guiltiest look on your face; *try* to be civil and not rummage through Tess's bank account, and in return I promise not to notice when your father gets drunk tonight and tries to ask me where I was stationed during the war."

But it was not Tess.

"The kitchen is closed until five," Alison said merrily to the young man who stood in the doorway with a puzzled expression, "but you're welcome to sit and have a cocktail with us in the meantime. You're about three hours too early for the rehearsal dinner, and I've already got a bridegroom, and our waitress has gotten herself lost and bitten by a snake somewhere in the woods between here and the kitchen, and spilled all the champagne, but don't let that spoil any of your fun. Are you free tomorrow morning? We could use an usher, or at least someone to sit on the groom's side." She turned to David. "Does the clerk's office have a groom's side? Never mind, you can have the whole city as the groom's side. If I'm going to have all the people, the least I can do is let you have a nice big side to be a groom in. I don't count his parents as people, you see"—that last line was directed to the man at the door, whom David couldn't fault for falling behind.

The man's expression grew even more puzzled (which David would not have thought possible only a minute ago), and he stammered out an apology. He had been looking for someone, and must have gotten the address wrong.

"Oh, don't mind that, I expect you were meant to get lost today. This here is the bridegroom," she said, gesturing at David. "This morning I frightened him. Tomorrow morning I'm going to marry him. Won't you have some champagne? Our waitress will be back any minute with three or four bottles of it. She's a very doughty waitress, and it would take more than a snakebite to delay her." But the man had been slowly edging out of the doorway during her speech, and by the time she got to the snakebite, he was gone, and they were alone again.

Alison gave a little laugh and pressed a kiss against David's hairline. He had the curious feeling that if he did not say something soon, he would lose the power of speech entirely.

"She's watched you," he said, "struggle like a specimen pinned and mounted to a card, when at any time she could have shaken out her handkerchief and let you have at least the stray coins that tumbled out." If he could not remove the whine entirely from his tone, he had at least managed to keep his voice steady, for the most part, and considered it a qualified hit.

She kissed him again. "What an ugly way to look at it."

"Has she even given you a wedding present?"

"You sound," Alison said, "alarmingly like a person who is asking for money."

"I don't mean that you should have asked her for it," he said. "I only meant that she's been in a position to do you some good, and I want to know why she hasn't—and why that doesn't seem to bother you."

"But the point is that Tess *hasn't* given me money, whether you think she ought to have or not," she said. "And she isn't stupid, which means that *at some point*, she's noticed that she has money and I haven't, which means that *at some point* she's thought about giving me some, and decided against it. So I could ask her for some, if I felt like embarrassing myself, and she'd arrive at the same decision, and then we'd be no differently situated than we were before, except I'd have been living with a woman I was ashamed to show my face to. My poor, grubby, impoverished face." And at this she pulled such a long and self-pitying expression that David could not help but smile at her.

"I think," he said, "if she really cared about you as much as she claims—"

"Perhaps you should go sit under Tess's window," she said, "and take your hat with you, and hold it out in front of you, stretched open wide, and carry a sign with the exact amount that you believe I am owed for performing the act

of friendship, and see if she is interested in dispensing lar-
gesse. Or settling her bill. You started out the day so well
too, David. I wonder if your hangover is operating in reverse,
and I should put you to bed until you get properly drunk
and fit for human society again."

"Why do I always feel as if I've insulted your mother
when I try to talk money with you?"

"I'm sure I have no idea. You could always try to stop
talking money with me, if you don't like the effect it produces. Stop pawing at me; you'll wrinkle my suit."

David dropped his hands reflexively, but she was smiling again, and he knew that the danger had passed. "And
tomorrow you'll marry me," he said, not quite believing it
still. "Tomorrow you'll marry me, and then you'll be married to me, and I'll take you out of the tower Tess has you
locked up in, and it won't matter if she tries to buy you the
moon, because I'll—"

"Tess would never try to give me the moon," she said,
frowning. "Tess would never give me something I couldn't
use."

"If you don't like the ring I bought you," he said, "I'll
buy you another one. Whatever kind you like. We'll throw
this one away." There was a very sharp sense of *imminence*
in his chest, somewhere between his lungs and a little lower
down. There was no other word for it; something, *something*
was going to happen, or already had.

"I like this ring," Alison said, and turned her hand to
look at it with the same cool, studied air of forgiveness she

always did. He would like to strike her, David thought suddenly. He would like to strike her and get up and leave, or fall at her feet and lay his head on her knees and beg until something happened. What that something might be, he could not quite imagine. "But you won't get any complaints from me if you feel inclined to buy me more jewelry."

"*Dar*ling," he said, and he kissed her.

* * *

The door did not open again, but Alison had seen something in the window, and snapped her handbag shut as she drew herself up from her chair. "That's Tess, just outside," she said, "and you look like you've just been having an argument, which is your own fault. I'll go out and talk to her. You stay here, and see if you can't convince that ancient mariner of a waitress to come back in and turn the lights on so Tess doesn't have to sit in the dark."

He'd kissed her hand then and tried to press it lightly to his cheek. "I'm sorry," he said. "I'm sorry, and I *do* like Tess, and I was a beast to ask about— Anyhow, I know it was never like that, with you, and I'll do anything you like, as long as you marry me; you can leave me here in the dark with the wind outside and I won't say a word until you come back, only if you'll marry me."

"I have your ring," Alison said, and she did not try to keep the impatience out of her voice. "You have a train ticket in your jacket pocket with my name on it, and there is a very unfriendly clerk at the marriage bureau who is counting on being unpleasant to the both of us at exactly ten o'clock tomorrow morning. I can't think of anything else I can do to convince you, but I hope at the least to find you sensible when I come back." She stepped lightly outside, closing the door behind her.

The waitress did not come back, and David had not felt right moving any farther away from the table than the entrance to the kitchen. The kitchen was full of shadows and flung his own voice back at him when he tried to halloo for attention. He did not have permission to go farther, so he went back and sat down.

There was no reason for him to open the door, because Alison was standing just outside, with Tess beside her, and she would open it and come back inside any minute. It was bad luck for a groom to see a bride on her wedding day; David thought, a trifle hysterically, that perhaps it was bad luck too for a groom to open any doors a bride kept closed the night before. David could just hear the low, warm tones of voices babbling on the other side of the door, and one belonged unmistakably to Alison. One of the voices paused to laugh, and the other swept darkly underneath it. The voices rose and fell together, bowing and nodding graciously to each other in turn, as if they were being continuously introduced. David closed his eyes and pictured Alison's long hands trailing after her words as she spoke.

Outside, the sun had vanished into the thick bank of clouds that banded the horizon, draining the street of every color but blue and darker blue. Hasty streetlights popped on in succession and threw bright pyramids of yellow against the sidewalk. A dozen footprints muttered past the doorway, but none stopped, and the door still did not open.

David pulled his cigarette case out from his jacket pocket and swung it all the way around the hinges until the sides met in reverse with a tinny little report. He distinctly heard his own name being pronounced in a feminine accent through the wall and jumped up from his seat, setting his ear against the door and straining to hear another "David, David." Alison was standing just outside—one of her hands was resting lightly on the knob, even now, ready to turn—and she had spoken his name, and Tess had heard it. Her face was already turned back in from the street—it turned, it was turning in his direction—and she was telling Tess that it was time to come inside.

He did not look out the window into the blurring street scene again, and he did not touch the handle of the door; for, he thought rather wildly to himself, if he were to try to look before they were ready to come inside, he might not see them at all; they might flash like birds down the street. He was seized with the notion that perhaps they had done so already, that the coiled, pleased voices hanging just out-side were all that remained of either of them, and that soon, soon, *now* they would dissolve into the thickening night, and he would never see them again.

He suddenly had a picture in his mind of himself, running out the front door and grabbing each passerby in turn, asking if they had please seen his wife, that he was expecting her. Then he saw them spreading their hands, smiling and refusing him gently, denying that she *was* his wife, that he had ever had a wife to begin with, that he had any right to be out on the street at all, collaring strangers and asking about a woman he had no part in. They might send him back inside, or throw him in prison for disturbing the peace, and so he did not move. She would come back, but not if he went out to find her, not if he stirred in the slightest from where he sat now. He would wait, and he would earn her. She had the ring. She had not liked it, but she wore it on her hand just the same, and that was sign enough. When she came back, he would never let her wear gloves again. He saw a horse's head, black-eyed and staring, fixed over the door, dripping and speechless.

He flipped his cigarette case open again and rested his chin against the door. There were still voices, softer now, falling every moment into a sweeter, deeper register he could not make out, and he wept a little at the loveliness of the vanishing sound. Soon—soon—*now* Alison was going to open the door and step inside. Tomorrow they were going to be married.

EIGHT

Some of Us Had Been Threatening Our Friend Mr. Toad

IT WAS A BRIGHT MORNING IN THE EARLY DAYS OF summer. Shortly after breakfast there came a knock at Mole's door. "See who it is, Mole, like a good fellow," Rat said. "I am attending to my egg."

Mole went to the door and uttered a cry of surprise. Then he threw the door open and announced (with an air of great importance), "Mr. Badger, welcome!"

"The hour has come!" declared Badger with great solemnity—or with as much solemnity as one could muster while wielding a boathook—as he stepped over the threshold.

"What hour?" asked Rat, looking over at the clock on the mantelpiece.

"*Whose* hour, you should rather say," replied Badger. "Why, Mr. Toad's hour! The hour of Toad! We said we would take him in hand as soon as the winter was well over, and we are going to take him in hand today!"

"Toad's hour—of *course*!" cried Mole in delight. "Hooray! I remember now! *We'll* teach him to be sensible!"

"How right you are," said Rat. "We'll rescue the poor, unhappy animal! We'll convert him—why, he'll be the most converted Toad there ever was by the time we're done with him."

"This very morning," continued Badger, settling into an armchair, "as I learned last night from a trustworthy source, another new and exceptionally powerful motorcar will arrive at Toad Hall. At this very moment, perhaps, Toad is busy readying himself to take a trip, without any of his friends. He may even now be preparing to run away from his friends who love him."

"Even now," Mole said, "he may be arraying himself in those disgusting motoring clothes which transform him from a comparatively bearable-looking Toad into an Object that throws any decent-minded person who comes across it into a violent fit."

"A *most* violent fit," Rat said. "Violent violent violent."

"Shall I bring a boathook, too?" Mole asked.

"I don't think so," Badger said. "You might bring a heavy blanket, or a tarpaulin, in case we have to Drown him."

"I don't believe we have ever Drowned Toad before," Mole said. "I suppose Helping is a bit like Drowning."

"Whatever you're going to bring along with you," Badger said, "you'd better fetch it quick. We must be up and about, before it is too late and Toad gets away without any Help at all. You two had better come with me to Toad Hall, and we can start the work of rescuing him."

"A *most* violent fit," Rat said again. "A violent violent fit."

They set off up the road at once, Badger leading the way and Rat dancing along behind, singing out, "A violent fit, a violent fit, a *most* violent violent violent fit," with every step. They made for a very merry crew.

"*I* should like to Help Toad first," Mole said. "Since I have known him the longest."

"Hello, fellows," Otter said, flinging his head above the riverbank and shaking the water from his muzzle. "What a noise you're making! All the world seems out on the river today. What news?"

"We are going to Help our friend Toad," Rat explained. "If I see him in his new motoring clothes, I am going to have a *most* violent fit. Then Mole is going to have a most violent fit. Then Badger is going to have a most—"

"Yes, I think I follow," Otter said politely. "May I join you?"

"We already have a boathook, a tarpaulin, a shovel, two steering poles, a mattock, a garden fork, and a luncheon basket," Badger said. "Have you got anything useful?"

"Just my net and fishing spear and a few lures," Otter said. "Will that do?"

"It might," Badger said.

"The more the merrier," Rat said.

"Can't be too prepared," Mole said. "Come along." Otter scampered up the bank, river water scattering off his back, and joined the line. Rat resumed his song as they walked to Toad Hall.

When they reached Toad Hall's carriage house they found—just as Badger had said they would—a shiny new motorcar, gleaming all over, painted blue, sitting just out front. As they drew near the front door it flew wide open and Mr. Toad came down the steps, already decked out in his motoring goggles, trim little brown cap, and duster, drawing on his driving gloves. He caught sight of them on the third step and stopped neatly in his tracks.

"Oh, hullo, fellows," he said. "I— Hullo. You're just in time—just in time to come with me for a jolly—to come for a jolly—for a—" The invitation faltered and fell away as he looked at all the friendly faces around him.

"Toad, what time do you suppose it is?" Mole asked.

"I don't know," Toad said. He smiled very brightly at each one of his friends. "I don't know. My head aches all of a sudden. I don't suppose I will go out today after all. I don't know."

"It's the hour of Toad!" Rat cried out merrily. "It's *your* hour, my precious darling, and we've all been having the most *violent* fits."

"Toad," Badger said, resting against his boathook, "what do you suppose we've come to Help you with?"

"I think my head aches too much to answer questions," Toad said, and if he was a little cross when he said it, we must excuse him, for his head *did* ache, a very great deal. "I think I'd better go back inside and lie down. Will you please excuse me?"

"No," Mole said.

"Yes," Rat said.

"I don't think—" Toad began.

"Listen to your friend Rat," Mole said.

"Listen to your friend Mole," Rat said.

"Thank you, Rat," Mole said.

"Thank *you*, Mole," Rat said.

"There are *so many* things we want to Help you with, Toad," said Badger.

Otter made a small noise in the back of his throat and shuffled gently up the stairs. "When are you going to invite us inside, Toad? We've come an awfully long way just to see you, and we've been carrying a great many heavy things."

Rat danced happily up to the chauffeur sitting in the driver's seat of the motorcar. "I'm afraid that *nobody* is going to need you today," he said. "Mr. Toad has changed his mind, and will not require the car. You needn't wait for him to change his mind, either. Mr. Toad never changes his mind but once."

"Think of what fun we'll have, Toady," Mole said,

"once you've quite gotten over this painful attack of yours. We'll take great care of everything for you until you're well again."

After a few minutes everyone—with the exception of the chauffeur, who was no longer wanted by anybody—went inside the house. Mole was a little out of breath, and Badger had the slightest of cuts over his right eye, but otherwise the entire rescue party was in fine spirits.

Toad spent a lot of time with his friends Badger, Mole, Rat, and Otter in the Wild Woods where they all lived. Here are a few of the things that happened to him.

The Noise

One day Toad went walking out in the Wild Woods to be by himself. As he was walking, he came to an empty place in the middle of the forest. But the middle of the empty place wasn't empty at all—there was a hole in the ground. And from inside the hole came a heavy sort of humming noise. Toad didn't mind the noise. He sat down at the edge of the hole, hung his head between his knees, and closed his eyes. He would only be by himself for a minute. He was never alone for very long in the Wild Woods, because the Wild Woods were full of Mr. Toad's friends, and you are never alone, as long as you have friends.

Then Toad said to himself: "That humming noise has to mean something. I've never heard a noise like that without something making it. If there is a humming noise, then something is *making* a humming noise, and the only thing I know of that makes a humming noise like that is a motor-car." So Toad dropped his legs over the side and swung round and grasped the edge of the hole with his forefeet, lowering himself bit by bit into the darkness.

Eventually Mole wandered into the clearing and took an interest. "Hello, Toad," he called down into the hole. "What are you doing down there?"

"I heard a noise," came a voice from very deep within the hole. "And I thought there might be something making the noise."

"I don't think you'll find anything down there but more noise," Mole said. "Why don't you climb back up to where I am?"

"I can do it," Toad said.

"No, you can't," Mole said in a sorrowful voice. "Your hands are tired. Your wrists are aching. Your head hurts. There's dirt in your mouth and the stones are cutting your feet. And the farther down you go, the worse it gets."

"I can do it," Toad said.

"I have to tell you something about the humming noise, Toad," Mole said. "It knows your name and doesn't like it. It knows who you are, and it doesn't like that either."

Toad kept climbing down.

"It knows that you're trying to get to it," Mole said, "and it likes that least of all. It's a gray sort of buzzing, isn't it, heavy and dull, and it makes your head spin, doesn't it?"

Toad said nothing, because his head was spinning. Mole was always right about that sort of thing.

"Why don't you come back up, where all your friends are here to see you?" Mole said.

"I haven't got any friends up there," Toad said.

"How can you say that," Rat asked, stepping out from behind Mole and peering down past the edge of the hole, "when you know we're the best friends you have in the whole world?"

"It's very sad that he would say that to us," Mole said to Rat.

"*Very* sad indeed," Rat said. "I'm going to cry unless Toad climbs out of that hole right now."

Finally Toad came back out. His head hurt, and his wrists were aching, and the stones cut his feet, and it didn't get any better when he reached the ground. And he was still hungry. He was so hungry that he fell over, and he tasted the dirt in his mouth.

"What a mess you look," Rat said.

"I'm hungry," said Toad. "I'm sorry. It's because I'm hungry."

"How can you be hungry," Mole said, "when you've just eaten every bite of the picnic lunch that Rat and I brought to share between ourselves?"

"I haven't had any picnic," Toad said, and tried to lift his arm to wipe his mouth. "I haven't had anything at all."

"It was very rude of you," Rat said, "to take all the

picnic lunch for yourself and not to offer even a little tiny bite to your friends."

"I'm sorry," Toad said to the dirt.

"We don't want you to be sorry," Mole said. "We just wish you would think of someone else once in a while. Toad, there's a picnic basket in that motorcar sitting at the bottom of that hole just below us. Why don't you climb down and bring it up?"

"All right," Toad said after a minute, and slowly lowered himself back down into the hole.

After Toad had begun to climb down, Rat shouted down after him, "Now, Toady, I don't want to give you pain—not after all you've been through already—but don't you see what a terrible ass you've been making of yourself? Handcuffed, imprisoned, starved, beaten, chased, jeered at, insulted, and terrified half out of your wits—where's the fun in that?"

"And all because you *must* go around stealing motorcars," Mole said. "You know you've never had anything but trouble from motorcars from the moment you first set eyes on one."

"If you *must* be mixed up with them," Rat said, "why *steal* them? Be a madman, if you think it's exciting; be bankrupt for a change, if you really set your mind to it; but why choose to be a convict? When are you going to be sensible and think of your friends, and try to be a credit to them? Do you suppose it's any pleasure for me, for instance, to hear people saying, as I go about, that I'm the chap that keeps company with gaolbirds?"

There was no answer from the hole at their feet except for the humming sound. Rat picked up a rock in his hand and weighed it thoughtfully. He shook his head.

"He brings it on himself," Mole said tragically.

Mr. Toad Gets a New House

It was a very commendable point of Toad's character that he never minded being jawed by any of his friends, who really did have his best interests at heart, and always forgave them after each episode. After the business with the humming sound in the hole ("And what a time we had taking care of you after *that*," Rat had said), Toad spent a few days lying very quietly on the floor with a cold washcloth over his eyes at Mole's house.

After about a week had passed, Toad began to speak of going home. "You've been quite right, Mole—I've been terribly conceited, I can see that now—but I'm going to be quite a good Toad from now on, and not go bothering with motorcars or holes in the ground or anything of the sort. I'm not so keen at all on motorcars now." He spoke very rapidly and without sitting up. "The fact is, I had the idea that I might take a nice quiet trip on a riverboat and— There, there! Don't take on so, Mole, and stamp and upset things; it was only an idea, and we won't talk any more about it now. We'll have our coffee, and a smoke, and then I'll go on home to Toad Hall, and back into my own clothes, and set things going again along the old lines. I've had quite enough of adventures, I can assure you. I shall lead a quiet, steady, respectable life, one that would make any of you proud to own me to anyone who asked. I shall potter about the property, making little improvements—nothing out of sorts, of course—doing a little gardening, and always having a bit of dinner ready for my friends when they come to see me, just as I used to in the good old days, before I got restless and wanted to *do* things."

"Go on home to Toad Hall?" asked Mole, quite excited. "What *are* you talking of? Do you mean to say you haven't heard?"

"Heard what?" asked Toad, turning over to face him. "Go on, dearest! Quick, don't spare me—what haven't I heard?"

Just then there came a knock at the door, and Mole jumped up to answer it. "Hello, Rat," he said (for it *was* Rat at the door). "Have you come here to tell Toad the bad news?"

"Hello, Mole," said Rat, very politely. "I thought you were out."

"Hello, Rat," Mole said again. "I don't believe that I am. I thought it was *you* who was out."

"As you like it, I'm sure," Rat said. "Won't you invite me in?"

"As *you* like it, I'm sure," Mole said, and stepped aside to make room for Rat, who immediately went into the kitchen and began boiling the water for tea.

"Rat," Mole said after a moment. "I have absolutely terrible news for Toad."

"Terrible news?"

"Just terrible news."

"I'm very sorry to hear that."

"I *thought* you'd be sorry to hear that, Rat," Mole said. "You're always very sympathetic."

"Is it the terrible news about his home?" Rat asked. "The terrible news about Toad Hall?"

"The very same terrible news," Mole said. "The very exact same terrible news about his home, Toad Hall."

"Oh, dear," Rat said, pouring two cups of tea, one for Mole and one for himself.

"Oh, dear," Mole said. "No sugar in mine, thanks."

Toad lifted himself up so he could see what was going on in the kitchen. "What has happened to Toad Hall?"

"I think it's *very* sad, what happened to Toad Hall," Mole said to Rat. "Won't you come and sit by the fire while we have our tea?"

"Thank you," Rat said, and the two of them took their tea back into the parlor where Toad was half twisted up from his pallet on the floor.

"I think it's very sad that our friend Toad doesn't have a house," Rat said. "I have a house, and you have a house, and Badger has a little house, too. Even Otter has a house of sorts. I think it is very sad that Toad is the only one who hasn't even the least little bit of a house."

"He used to have a house," Mole said. "A very fine one too, was Toad Hall."

"Will someone *please* tell me what has happened to Toad Hall," Toad said desperately.

"Oh," said Mole, "you haven't heard what's happened to Toad Hall? Well, it was a good deal talked about down here, naturally—not only along the riverbanks, but even in the Wild Woods."

"Very strange, your not hearing of it," Rat said, "how They went and took Toad Hall, while you've been so sick lately."

"They made arrangements, while you were ill," Mole said. "They said anyone as sick in the head as you have been was not likely to return home anytime soon—and you must admit They had a point, for you *have* been distressing us all terribly with your behavior lately—and They decided They had better move Their things into Toad Hall, and sleep there, and make sure everything was ready for you when you turned up, if you ever turned up."

Toad only nodded.

"If you ever turn up," Rat said, "I expect They will still be there waiting for you. Some of Them came in through the carriage drive, and some of Them came in through the kitchens and the gardens, and some of Them came in through the French windows that open onto the lawn, and I expect all of Them are still there waiting for you."

"People took sides about it," Mole said, "naturally. I think it was a terrible shame, no matter *what* people say about you, no matter how often folks said you were never coming back."

"Never, never, never coming back," Rat agreed. "This is excellent tea, Mole."

"Thank yourself," Mole said. "You made it."

"So I did," Rat said, taking another sip.

"But we knew you would be back to your old self in no time," Mole said to Toad after a few minutes' silence, "and that you would be eager to go back to Toad Hall and clear Them out, even if no one else went with you, and you had to creep back all by yourself in the darkness to whatever met you behind your own front doors."

"*We* knew," Rat agreed. "We knew you'd as good as promised to go back and clear Them out."

"But he *hasn't* gone back and cleared Them out, has he, Rat?" Mole asked.

"No, Mole," Rat said slowly, "come to think of it, he hasn't. Toad hasn't kept his promise at all. Why do you suppose that is?" And he turned to ask him, but Toad was nowhere to be seen. "Toad," Rat said. "Where have you got to, and why haven't you kept your promise?"

Mole jerked his head toward the kitchen. "Toad is hiding among the pots and pans," he said. "I expect he is hiding because he is so ashamed of being a coward."

"Toad," Rat called, "are you hiding among the pots and pans?"

"Toad," Mole said, "why would you rather be with the pots and pans than with your friends? Come out and have a visit with us."

After a moment, the cupboard door opened, and Toad crept out. He crawled along the floor until he was back at Mole's feet.

"Toad," Mole said sternly, "you promised to go back and clear Toad Hall of all your enemies who are living there, sleeping in your beds and drinking your tea. Why haven't you done it?"

"Toad," Rat said, "did you mean it when you promised you would go back and clear out Toad Hall, or were you telling a lie?"

"I didn't," Toad said. "Or, I mean, I didn't tell a lie or make a promise either. I didn't even know there was anybody else in my house until you told me, just now."

"At the very least," Mole said in an injured tone, "I would think you would want to go back to Toad Hall so you could invite Rat and myself over for tea, after all the hospitality I've shown you since you've been so ill."

"I would *so* like to have tea," Rat said, setting down his cup. "I haven't had any tea in the longest time, and Mole hasn't either—he's been too busy worrying himself over you."

"Toad," Mole said, "you are a very good friend, only I wish you would tell the truth, because you always feel so sick when you tell lies. You *did* promise you would sweep Toad Hall clear of all your enemies, and I think it's high time you got up off my parlor floor and went home to find out what was living there."

"I know I didn't," Toad said. "I know I didn't."

"Then why do you feel so sick right now?" Mole asked.

"I don't," Toad said. "I don't feel sick, I don't, I don't."

"Then why can't you stand back up?" Mole said. "And why does your head feel so funny?"

"I don't know," Toad said. "Maybe—"

"I think you are telling lies again. I think you would feel better if you told us the truth. Would you like to feel better?"

"Yes," Toad said in a small misery voice.

"Would you like to be able to get up again?" Mole asked.

"Yes," Toad said.

"I can't hear you when you mumble, Toad," Mole said. "Did you say yes?"

"Yes," said Toad, turning his head.

"I would like it if you felt better and could get up again," Mole said. "Wouldn't you, Rat? Wouldn't we all like it if Toad would tell us the truth and feel better?"

"*I* would," Rat said.

"We both want you to feel better," Mole said. "It makes us sick too when you tell lies."

"I feel terribly sick," Rat said, pouring himself another cup. "Every time Toad tells a lie, I feel sick."

"I'm sorry I told you a lie, Rat," Toad said.

"Do you forgive him, Rat?" Mole said.

"I forgive him," Rat said. "I forgive you, Toad."

"Are you going to go to Toad Hall, and see all of Them who have been living there and saying such hateful things about you, and about all the things they would like to do to you if they got their hands on you, and keep your promise, Toad?" Mole asked. "You don't have to say yes again if it hurts to talk. You can just nod."

Toad nodded.

"Are you going to start now?" Mole asked.

Toad nodded.

"Do you need help getting up, so you can start keeping your promise?" Mole asked.

Toad nodded, and his friends helped him get up. He only wobbled a little as he went out the front door.

NINE

Cast Your Bread Upon the Waters

AQUINAS SAYS PASSION DESERVES NEITHER PRAISE nor blame, and I have no quarrel with that. If *acedia*, that noonday demon, is a kind of passion—a species of sadness, as the Damascene says—then it is no sin in itself. Yet surely passions can be blameworthy when attached to unworthy objects. Surely the *immoderation* of such spiritual torpor, if left unchecked, is, if not yet full sin in bloom, at least the error that may in time lead to sin. For our story, it all led to sin in the end, and it all began with the listlessness and self-forgetting that comes not from God.

* * *

The woman, in this instance, was wicked, and the man was stupid. That is not always the case between women and men, but that is how it ever was with the two of them. There came a great wickedness out of a small fault; I saw it with my own eyes. Together they committed a wickedness that has left me with six children to bring up in my old age, when I should be preparing myself for a crown and glory. Had I known what would come of it, I would have smothered Johnnie Croy in his crib before he ever grew into a man. But I never had the right to kill him until he sinned a great sin, of course.

There are six eternal sins that defy the Holy Ghost and merit Hell: Despair, or believing that one's own sin is more powerful than divine grace; Presumption, seeking pardon without repentance or glory without worthiness; Resistance, to truth; Envy of the spiritual glory of a brother or resenting the increase of grace in the world; Impenitence, or not repenting of a sin already committed; Obstinacy, willfully intending to grow further in sin.

Johnnie was tall and well formed, and people liked to look at him and to listen to him talk. He had a fine voice, warm and rumbling, and it made you smile to hear it. I liked him fine myself, but I did not mistake any of his talents for virtue. The Lord sees not as man sees, but looks on the heart.

He claimed to have first seen the woman when he was out collecting driftwood, which certainly may have been true. He had heard her singing before he saw her, and of course her voice was so piercing and sweet and otherworldly that he had to abandon his labor and listen to her. Well, I call that sloth, however pretty the music. She was sitting on a rock way out past the tide line and combing her long hair— because her people neither work nor pray and have endless time for vanities.

You will think me grim, and an enemy of joy, to begrudge my son a snatch of music or my son's love of her pretty hair. Well, I saw what came of it. I like music and pretty things as much as anyone, within reason, but I also need drift-wood more than I need stories of invisible concerts. We sell abstract driftwood sculptures to mainlanders, who love buying sticks of wood shaped to look vaguely like horses' heads, and chairs no one can sit in, and great big knobby burls to put on their coffee tables. They especially like buy-ing them from flinty old islanders and their good-looking sons, and since fishing doesn't bring in what it used to, we end up needing a lot of driftwood.

So instead of collecting driftwood or fishing or looking to his chores, my good-looking son spent the afternoon watching a damp woman groom herself on a rock. Like jet her hair was, which grew all the way down to the back of her knees, and her eyes were fine, and my good-looking son, who had already committed the sin of sloth, grew obstinate, and fully intended to sin again. A *woman* is not a sin, mind, but *this* woman was, so of course my son came home and told me he could not love anyone else but her. "You don't have to love anyone else if you haven't a mind to," I said, "but I'd be much obliged if you could love her and bring home driftwood at the same time."

"How can you talk of driftwood when my heart lies somewhere in the sea?" he said. "Don't speak to me of driftwood; I care nothing for it."

"Well, if it comes to that," I said mildly, "I don't much like it myself, but I do enjoy being able to pay for things like tea and whisky and tobacco when I go to the grocer's; call it an old islander's habit and indulge me."

"I kissed her," he said. "I went out past the tide line, and I waited until she put down her comb, and I put my arms around her and I kissed her."

"Did you?" I said.

"She hit me for it," he said, trying to sound sheepish. "Right in the jaw." Which isn't a very smart place to hit a man—hurts like hitting another fist.

"What did you do then?" I asked.

"I apologized," he said. "Then I stole her comb." So I added theft to his list of offenses.

"You'll keep the priest busy, at least, if not yourself," I said.

He went on to say that she had begged for the return of the comb, which he showed me; its teeth were an evil gray-green color and I misliked it. She had jumped into the water and raged at him, and told him that to lose her comb was a great shame, and that she could not return to her accursed people who lived underneath the waves without it. Johnnie's answer to that was that she should not return to them, but come home and live with him (that it was not his home to offer but mine had presumably not troubled him). "For," said he, "there is no point in ever trying to love someone else now."

"No point at all," I agreed.

But she would not come home with him, which showed she had some sense, and said she could not abide our black rain or smoky huts, the snow in winter, and the hot sun in summer, and told him to come with her instead.

"Which you did not do," I said.

"Which I did not do," he said. "I told her my home was not a hut, but had several rooms in it, and land and sheep besides, and that I had also a boat, a hand-mirror, a big bed, and some cash in the mattress, and that I would give her anything else she wanted. But she would not come with me."

She called herself Gem-de-Lovely, which was the stupidest name I had ever yet heard, and she countered his offer with the promise of a white palace built under the caves in the sea, and freedom from both sunshine and wind, and all sorts of creatures he had never seen but might have dominion over—if he would come with her and let her drown him and be her man. She would have had the right to drown him, either for the unlawful taking of her comb, or for the unlawful taking of a kiss. My son was not quite so stupid as to agree to that, but he was stupid enough to sit on that rock for another hour and stare at her, and let her stare at him, and they both loved each other all the more for the looking. He was a very good-looking man.

Eventually, I suppose she did tire of just looking at him, even as handsome as he was, and she swam farther out, crying, "Alas, alas, my lovely comb. Alas, alas, my lovely man," and then she was gone.

"So now I want you to help me catch her," he said.

"It would be a wicked catching," I said to him, "and the keeping of her more wicked still." But he did not mind. "If you take an unbaptized wife, I cannot help you, whatever comes after." But he did not mind that either.

* * *

He kept the comb in his room, and went about his work in a daze, and he would not speak to any of the local girls who used to keep him from his labors. The next week he came into my study as I was going over the accounts and began to speak without leave.

"I saw her again last night," he said. "Gem-de-Lovely. She was sitting at the foot of my bed."

"I congratulate you," I said. "She has caught herself for you, and you have no need of my help."

"She was a vision," he said, as if I had not spoken at all. "The most beautiful creature anyone has ever seen—you will agree on this, if nothing else, when you see her—and she loves me. She was so beautiful I thought she might be an angel."

"Did you pray, when you thought you had seen one?"

"I tried to," he said. "I tried to offer up a prayer of thanks, but I found that I could not. I had forgotten every prayer I had ever learned."

As the one who had taught him every prayer he ever knew, I did not especially like that. "Can you remember one now?"

"I will," he said. "I will pray every morning and evening, once I have her."

"One prayer now would be better than a hundred tomorrow," I said.

"You are likely right," he said, "but you are also interrupting my story. She came back to ask me to return her comb, which I had under my pillow, and which I could not give her. For if she does not marry me, I will die, and I wish to be buried with it. Then she asked, if I would not return the comb, if I would not change my mind and live with her under the sea, and I told her I could not, but begged her to visit my grave when I perished from the wanting of her."

"You two are never at a loss for conversation, at least," I said.

"Then," he continued, "she made me a new offer."

I put down my pen. "Did she," I said.

"She did," he said. "A fair one, too. She said she loved me, and that she would be my wife and live here with me for seven years, if I would swear to come to her palace under the sea with all that was mine at the end of them."

"Naturally, you agreed."

Johnnie smiled. He was terribly beautiful when he smiled, and I loved to see him do it. "I threw myself down on my knees, and I promised all that and more."

* * *

So that was settled, then. That same week they were married. She let the priest do it, which surprised me. I would not have thought she would be able to stand in the church and hear a bible spoken over her. But she was made of strong stuff, and smiled at everyone, and only shivered a little when the priest made the sign of the cross over her. The two of them together were as lovely as the sun over the sea. Pearls as big as fists studded her hair.

And so for seven years she lived with my Johnnie as his wife—lived with *us* as Johnnie's wife. I said nothing, as it was a lawful marriage, but cataloged their sins and watched my son's beautiful face for signs of repentance, and watched his wife's beautiful face for signs of pity. And things went well, as long as she was with us. The fish ran as they hadn't in years, the sheep got fat, a man from the government came out and installed a wind turbine at the end of the grazing field, the grocer got her checks on time. Gem-de-Lovely did not work, and neither did Johnnie, and so the additional labor fell on me. I found their chores came as easily to me as my own; I have never minded work. Some in the neighborhood might fault me for the sin of omission—might say I had the opportunity to tear up wickedness by the root and did not act—but I say I gave them both seven years' opportunity to choose grace. That they did not seek it was a great grief to me.

They had six children, all healthy, all carrying their parents' promise of beauty. Johnnie kept the gray-green comb on the mantelpiece over the fireplace in the kitchen, and often I would catch him staring at it. I suppose sometimes I stared at it, too.

So the seven years came to an end, and Johnnie had not repented of his ill-gotten wife, nor of his heretical promise, and she was still determined to drown him. A faraway look came to her beautiful eyes, and she was ever smiling and looking out the window toward the sea. Johnnie took to varnishing the fishing boat down by the slip, the first honest work I'd seen from him in years. Some afternoons he took the children with him, and sailed out and around the bay. He always had at least the decency to look sheepish after those trips.

Seven years on God's soil, and after that a brief, drowned life with a flooded, faithless people, with no hope of salvation or eternity thereafter; this was the bargain Johnnie thought fair, and meant to give his children as inheritance besides. He was ever careless with his own soul, but now he grew careless with theirs. I had baptized the children each myself in secret after they had been born, although I suspect I always knew that would not do much good when the time came. I had baptized Johnnie too, for all the good it had done him.

On the last night of their marriage, I arose from my bed and fashioned a little cross out of old radio coils. I buried it in the embers of the kitchen fire until it glowed red, and I went into the children's room and pulled back the covers from their beds. I pressed the cross between each of their shoulder blades in turn, oldest to youngest. Had they been awake, they likely would have screeched like anything, but I had put enough Veronal in their milk at supper that they would not have stirred if the world were ending. There would be enough time for screaming in the morning, if they thought it would help ease the pain. If Johnnie was determined to be drowned, that was his affair, but he would not drag six little souls with him, to grow up in dark and dripping sea caves with a thief for a father and a murderer for a mother.

I'd given Johnnie the Veronal too, and he lolled back and forth as I tied his hands and feet. Our family has always raised sheep; branding and binding were not new to me. It was a heavy thing, to carry my son out to the boat and put him in it. He was the only son I ever had, and he was the most beautiful thing I have ever seen, even now. I had not bothered to drug Gem-de-Lovely. I grabbed the fire iron from the hearth and thrust the point into the hollow of her collarbone. She woke up choking on her throat's blood and glaring furiously at me.

"Come with me," I told her, and kept her in front of me as we went down the stairs. She clutched at her bleeding neck with one hand and tried to open the door to the children's room with the other. I had thought of that, too; the door was covered in dozens more of the wire crosses I had made. She shook her head and wept. I prodded her in the small of the back and walked with her toward the little boat tied up at the launch.

"Your man is waiting for you," I said. "Get in the boat."

"Give me my children," she said.

"You are lucky I have not cut off all the hair on your head," I said. "Trouble me again and I will; I have scissors in my pocket."

"Give me my children," she said, falling to her knees in the sand and clasping my feet.

"Your bargain was never with them," I said. "You will have Johnnie, and you will have your comb, and you will go home, and I will call that fair."

"Alas, alas, for my fine children!" she cried. "Alas, that I must leave them to live and die on dry land!"

Well, she would have gone on like that for who knows how long if no one had stopped her, so I jabbed her with the fire iron. "Get in the boat," I said. She snapped her mouth closed and stared at me instead. Then I jabbed her again, once in the leg and once in the side, and she must not have liked that so well, because she shook her head something fierce at me. But she also started walking back toward the sea. She had gray blood like a squid, and it pulsed all over her dress as she swung her leg over the side and stepped into the boat.

So I had them both in the boat then, Gem-de-Lovely, who was wicked, and Johnnie Croy, who was stupid, and upstairs sleeping all six of their children, safe and whole. Johnnie lay quietly on the floor of the boat. I think he was awake then. His mouth hung a little open and he did not look at me, nor move or speak. The woman looked at me still, and so I looked back at her, and would for as long as she remained in sight. I took her comb out of my pocket and set it down next to her.

"Woman," I said, "I never liked you." I jabbed the fire iron through the side of her neck, piercing the pulse. It seemed like enough to kill her, although of course one never knows with creatures. It was just as likely that as soon as she touched seawater, all her wounds would close over like a starfish, and she'd sprout new and harder skin, and new and longer limbs.

"And I," she said to me, glaring as hard as she could (if she'd had a fire iron then herself, I'd have been in terrible trouble), "I have never liked you, nor ever will." Her mouth was full of that gray blood, and it dripped down her chin as she talked.

"A whip for a horse," I said, "a bridle for a donkey, and a rod for the back of fools." I don't know why I warned her next, but I did. "I'm going to speak a bible over you now," I told her. "Brace yourself."

She lifted a hand and tried to smile. "At present, I can do little more than listen and bleed." Well, that suited me fine, too. I don't know why I felt like she deserved a warning now. I certainly hadn't spared her much. But I'll take credit for a little mercy, if anyone sees fit to add it to my glory. I made the cross over her first, then him. They both shuddered under the sign of it.

"Lord God," I said, "you gathered all the oceans into a single place; at your command the waters dry up and the rivers disappear. You have set up the shore as the boundary of the sea; though the waves toss, they cannot prevail, and though they roar, they cannot pass over it. We commit the

earthly remains of my son, Johnnie, to the deep, and we commit this woman, too. Grant them a sure sinking, and a final
baptism, and do not let them pass back over the shore, not
even when the sea gives up her dead in the final resurrection."

I knelt down at the side of the boat next to my son, who
would not look at me, and I stroked his hair. "You should
never have taken her comb," I said to him.

The book of Matthew, chapter eighteen: Jesus said to
the disciples, "Woe unto the world because of offenses, for
it must needs be that offenses come, but woe to that man by
whom the offense cometh. Better that a millstone were
hanged about his neck, and he cast into the sea, than that
he should offend one of those little ones." Well, I know my
scripture, and I know what offends me, and I knew which
man by whom the offense had come.

"If thy hand or thy foot offend thee, cut them off," I said
to Johnnie, "and cast them from thee: it is better to enter into
life halted or maimed, rather than having two hands or two
feet to be cast into everlasting fire. And if thine eye offend
thee, pluck it out, and cast it from thee. Johnnie, thine eye
has offended thee."

Well. He didn't like that, but he could hardly disagree
with it either. He *would* have taken those children with him.
I call that offense to little ones, and I had my knife, so I used
it. "Tell me which one you wish to keep, and I'll spare it," I
said to him. He didn't want to answer me, so I waited. "I
have saved you from the worst of sins," I said. "Let me help
a bit more, and do not make me send my only son full-blind

to his death in the sea." He waited another minute, then jerked his head to the right, and I thanked him.

As he had used it for theft and unlawful gain, and lusts of the flesh, and shirking his duty—as he would have used it to take his children to drown with him—I cut off the left hand of Johnnie Croy. As he had used it to look too long in the wrong direction, I cut out his left eye, too.

But as he had *not* taken the children, I left him his right hand and the right eye in his head. The rest I threw into the sea. All the while he said nothing, only groaned, while his wife bled and glared beside him. When it was finished, he turned his face from me, and rested his head on his good arm, and seemed to fall back asleep.

Then I shoved the boat with my foot and watched it float out across the water for a long time. After a while I could no longer see the woman's face, although I have no doubt it was still turned toward me. She watched me, I think, for as long as she could. She may have tried to speak her own bible back at me, or she may have only gurgled. I don't know. I did not hear her again. Eventually the sun came up. I took my fire iron and I went home to raise up those six children. My son Johnnie was very beautiful, and I loved him.

TEN

The Frog's Princess

I N AN OLD TIME, IN AN OLD COUNTRY, THERE LIVED A man whose daughters were all beautiful and unlucky. To be beautiful in this place was to be noticed; it was for this reason his daughters were so remarkably unlucky. Here people prayed to be forgotten, and they prayed with their faces to the floor.

It was the man's youngest daughter who was the unluck-iest of all. He was so beautiful that the sun herself noticed and had in fact fallen quite in love with him, and never let her rays stray from his face for even a moment while she hung above the rim of the world. So the youngest daughter slept with his face jammed into a pillow, and with coverlets piled over his head, but the sun would not let him sleep unnoticed. Every day she found him, and every day she woke him while everyone else was still asleep. Beauty is never private.

"Beauty does not belong exclusively to you," the man told his daughters. "Beauty is a public good, and you are responsible for it."

"What does that mean, exactly?" the youngest daughter asked. The sun burned hot on his forehead.

"It means—in a sense—that according to a certain understanding you belong to everyone," the man said. (The man himself was not beautiful, but he was often covered in beautiful objects, which he considered to amount, more or less, to the same thing.)

"By that reasoning," his daughter said, "I belong at least partly to myself. Certainly at least as much as I belong to anybody else."

"Don't be clever," his father said. "Go and play outside, where people can see you."

In this country, a daughter was least safe at the age when *they* wished to play while *other* people wished to notice them. When people wanted to notice him, the man's youngest daughter had learned, nothing could talk them out of it. They noticed, then they offered remark, and then they acted, always in that order.

The land near the man's house was very old and thickly

wooded. In this forest, beneath a linden tree, there was a well full of standing water. In the heat of the day, when the sun's attentions became unbearable, the man's youngest daughter would run across the highway and into the woods, where the trees stood so close together that almost no light reached the ground.

(Obviously *some* light did reach the ground. Otherwise how else could a well have possibly been built there? It had by this time been abandoned, but in order for a well to be abandoned, it must first have been built. There had once been enough light in the woods to make a well feasible there, and enough light now for a brackish layer of organic material to have wrapped long gray-green fingers around it. Enough light too, for the layer to spread itself over old tree throws and root pits, given sufficient time. So let us say there was light sufficient for our present purposes.)

So that was where the youngest daughter went, generally, when he did not feel disposed to belong to anyone, and he would sit at the edge of the well in a spot where the brackish layer had not yet thrown down roots. He would take with him a golden ball, as round and as yellow as the sun. He would throw it straight up in the air, then catch it when it came down; he never threw it in any other direction. In this way, he might throw and catch and fling away the sun as easily as he liked. It was his favorite pastime, and he never tired of it.

On this day, it happened that he threw the golden ball so high into the branches overhead that it disappeared into the spreading darkness, only to drop suddenly far to the left of him and vanish with a smothering sound into the well. He leaned over the edge and looked down, but the water was so dark, and the well so deep, that he could not see the slightest sign that anything had ever been there but scum and mosquitoes. If anyone had tried to console him in that moment, he would have sunk down onto the stone and refused them, but no one did, so he continued to lean over the well, looking down.

(You may be wondering why he did not try to fish the ball out of the well himself; you are only wondering this because you have not seen the well with your own eyes. The well's only redeeming feature was its solitude. The water within had not run for years and smelled like old coins.)

Also, he was not stupid, and knew better than to dive into water he didn't know how deep, when there was only one way in or out. Eventually, however, someone came along and noticed his crying (as someone generally did), and called out to him (as someone generally did after noticing him): "What is the matter with you? Yours is a face too beautiful for tears." Which was patently untrue, but people said it just the same. He looked around to find the voice and saw that a frog had thrust its flat, wet head out of the well. The frog looked like a calf's heart with a mouth slit across it.

"Oh, it's you," he said. "I was crying because I lost something that I love."

"*Are* crying," the frog said. "You haven't stopped yet." Which was a fair thing to point out, if slightly unkind. "Be still, and stop crying—or carry on crying for as long as you like, I suppose. Whichever you prefer, only, I can help you find it."

"But you don't know what I've lost," he said.

"Oh," the frog said vaguely, "didn't you mention it?"

"I don't believe I did. I'm sure I didn't, actually."

"Tell me what it was, then," the frog said, "or better still, I can simply tell *you* what's in this well that wasn't here an hour ago, and you can tell me if it belonged to you."

"Oh," he said.

"Yes, *oh*," the frog said. "I can help you, but what will you give me if I bring you back your plaything?"

"But I did not ask you to help me," he said, "so why should I promise you anything?"

"You are sitting on my well," said the frog. "You are beautiful, and you are crying, and I saw you before anyone else did; that is almost the same thing as asking, or being asked, anyhow." The frog brushed its long, thumbless hand over his, and the man's youngest daughter had no answer for that.

"I don't know what I should promise you," he said. "You can have anything else that I own. I could bring you something, if there was something that you wanted, and that you could not get for yourself, I suppose. My chain of office that my father gave me." That was all he could think to offer.

The frog said, "Keep your boyish treasures—I don't want them, nor is there anything you can fetch for me I could not get myself. I do not need an errand boy. But if you will accept me as a companion, and let me sit next to you at your father's table, and eat from the plate you eat from, and drink from your cup, and sleep in your bed; if you would promise this to me, then I'll dive back into the well and bring your golden ball back to you."

"Yi-i-i-i-ikes," the boy said slowly. He thought of his father's words: *You are responsible for your beauty.* "Well," he said. "I could promise all this to you, if you brought it back to me." He hoped that maybe the frog was joking, although he had no reason to believe it was; people rarely joked with him. He thought, as he often did before making a promise, that perhaps he would not have to keep it, or that maybe the promise would not be so bad in the keeping as it had been in the making.

But no one was ever joking when they asked him to make a promise, and everyone always remembered when he owed them something. And it should be remembered here that he was the *youngest* daughter, after all, and had not yet learned as much about being a daughter as some of the others. At any rate, as soon as the frog heard him say yes, it stopped listening to him and dove back into the water, a dark clot darting swiftly under the surface, until it disappeared from sight entirely.

A few minutes later the frog paddled up to the edge of the well with the golden ball bulging between its thin lips and spat it out onto the grass. Its tongue was a livid purple and bulged out of its mouth. But the youngest daughter was too happy to pay much attention to how the frog looked. He was so relieved, in fact, that he picked up the ball immediately and ran for home.

"Wait," said the frog, wheezing and dripping. "Take me along. I cannot run as fast as you can; that is not my fault but yours." But he could no longer hear the frog, and quickly forgot about it and what it had done for him in the forest.

The next day the youngest daughter was sitting at the table with his father and all his sisters, when something with a lipless mouth and thumbless hands hauled itself up the front steps of the house. It knocked on the door and called out, "Daughter, youngest, open the door for me!" So he ran to see who it was, and opened the door wide to see the frog sitting there, panting from the strain of crawling up the stairs. He slammed the door shut and sat back down at the table. His father saw his face and asked, "Why are you so distressed, and who was at the door?"

"It was a frog," he said. Then: "We are going to have to wash the front steps."

"Did someone knock on our front door and leave a frog there," his father asked, "or did the frog knock and expect to be let in?"

"Well," his youngest daughter said. "I think it wanted to be let in."

"I did not ask what the frog wanted," his father said. "I asked if the frog *expected* to be let in." All the other daughters had stopped pretending to eat at this point and stared in open excitement at the prospect of watching one of their number get into trouble.

"Well," his daughter said. "Only—yesterday, when I was sitting near the well in the forest, my golden ball fell into the water."

"Sitting near the well, or on it?"

"On it, Father. Sitting on it, and my golden ball fell into the water, and I was crying over it, and I was crying *so* much that the frog brought it back to me, and because it insisted on repayment, I promised him that he could be my companion, but I did not think it would be possible for the frog to leave the well, because—don't frogs *have* to live in the water? And now it is sitting outside the door and wants to come in."

"If you were sitting on the well and not just near it," his father said, "then you must keep your promise." Just then there came another knock at the door.

"But I did not really promise it," the youngest daughter said. "It made the promise for me, and to itself, and I did not really ask it to get the ball. It volunteered." He scrunched down low in his seat, too late to escape notice. He really was a very unlucky daughter.

His father said only: "You should not have sat on a well that was not yours. Go and open the door, and let the frog in."

He went back to the door and opened it, and the frog hopped inside, then followed him back to his chair. It sat at his feet a moment and then said, "Lift me up next to you." He did not move until his father insisted. Then he did it.

The frog sat next to his hand on the table, and said,

"Now push your plate closer to me, so we can eat together."
Its breath smelled like old coins, and the youngest daughter
shuddered but brought the plate closer. The frog did not
mind that he shuddered, only that he did as instructed.
Everyone else could see that he did not want to eat, but no
one said anything, as they were not the ones in trouble. The
frog ate everything with a hearty appetite.

"Eat," his father said, and he ate, too.

Finally the frog said: "I have eaten everything I wanted
to eat. Now I am tired. Carry me to your room and put me
in your bed, so that we can go to sleep."

The man's youngest daughter began to cry. This time
no one said anything about his being too beautiful for tears.
"Maybe you would prefer a little bed of your own," he
said. "Mine is—starched, and dry, and you might not be com-
fortable in something so clean. I could make you a little nest,
or put some water in a bucket nearby, or—"

"Put me in between your knees," the frog said. "I will
be warm there, and the only thing that will get dirty is you,
and you can wash."

At this the youngest daughter shook his head and shrank
back in his seat. His father grew angry and said, "You took
help when it was offered, and you flinch now at repayment;
do not make use of someone else's property, and do not offer
someone your beauty, if you do not intend to repay them in
kind."

Now the youngest daughter wished that he could throw
his ball back in the well and never see it again. "I would

rather have a punishment than receive a favor like this again," he said.

"*Rather* all you like," his father said, "only, stop making me tell you to do what you already know. I have other daughters to manage, not only you."

So the youngest daughter picked up the frog with two fingers and held it out before him. His skin puckered wherever it touched him. "What about my chores?" he asked, knowing full well he was stalling.

"You have your chore before you," his father said. "Everything else can wait."

He carried the frog upstairs and set it in a corner of his room, where it sat and stared at him. Next he got into bed without looking at it, but as he was lying under the blankets, it came creeping up to the foot of the bed. The frog said, "I am tired, and I want to sleep, too. Pick me up, and put me in bed with you, or I'll tell your father."

This was one request too many, and the youngest daughter became violently angry and shook all over. He threw back the blankets, picked up the frog, and flung it against the wall as hard as he could. "*Here* is your payment, and *here* is your thanks—now keep your peace!" The frog slid down to the floor and began to croak. It croaked louder and louder until his father filled the doorway, and picked the frog up himself, and placed it in bed with his daughter. Then he left, closing the door behind him without saying a word.

The frog was all the softer for having been thrown

against the wall. It crawled underneath his legs, cold and close, and pressed a lipless kiss against the back of his knees. The daughter wished that all his skin was dead and gone. By and by the frog fell asleep, and the boy lay awake and staring all night, and for many nights afterward. He was very unlucky.

ELEVEN

Good Fences Make Good Neighbors

ONCE THERE WAS A FISHERMAN WHO LIVED WITH his friend, and they lived quite happily together in a little house by the sea. Every day he went out and fished, and every night he came home to his friend and they had dinner together. One day the fisherman went out and cast his hook as far as it would go. It sank down and down and when he pulled it back out, he saw that he had caught a large flounder.

The flounder said, "Fisherman, let me go. I am not an ordinary flounder; I am something else."

"Could you be more specific?" the fisherman said. " 'Something else' could mean anything."

"That's a very personal question," said the flounder.

"More personal than being eaten?"

"That is a fair point," the flounder said. "I am not a fish at all, but the son of someone very powerful. I have fallen under an enchantment through no fault of my own. It will do you no good to eat me; I would turn to ashes in your mouth."

"A fish might say that," the fisherman said.

"A fish might," the flounder agreed, "but a man might say it, too. Put me back in the water. Let me go, and I promise I'll do something for you that no one else can do."

"I'll have to speak with my friend first," the fisherman said. "I cannot think of anything I want at present."

"That is your right," the flounder said, and the fisherman slid the hook out from its mouth and let it sink back into the water, trailing blood behind it.

* * *

The fisherman went home to his friend, who was lying in bed with the lights turned off. His friend said, "What did you catch today?"

"Nothing," the fisherman said. "Well, I caught a flounder, but it told me that it was not a flounder at all, but the son of someone very powerful and important, so I put him back."

"Did he promise you anything?" his friend asked.

"He said he would give me something no one else could

grant," the fisherman said, "but I couldn't think of anything I wanted at present, so I didn't ask."

His friend said nothing, and the fisherman knew that he had said the wrong thing.

"My friend," the fisherman said, "are you feeling quite well?"

His friend said: "This is why people don't like helping you."

"People don't like helping me?" the fisherman said.

"They do not," his friend said. "This is why you are lucky to have me."

"I didn't know that," the fisherman said.

"You are lucky," his friend said again, "that I am here to tell you these things. You should have asked for a better house; I am ashamed to let people see how we live here together."

"You are?" the fisherman said.

"I have always been ashamed of it," said his friend.

"I am sorry," the fisherman said.

"Do not be sorry," his friend said. "Go and do something about it."

"Now?" the fisherman said. "It is dark out."

"In the morning, then," his friend said, turning over to face the wall. "We might as well go to sleep now, since you have brought home nothing for us to eat." So they went to sleep, and in the morning the fisherman went back out to the sea, and baited his hook, and waited for the flounder to come back.

The flounder swam up to his boat and poked its head out of the water. "What did your friend say, then?"

"Oh," said the fisherman, a little embarrassed. "My friend thinks that we should have a better house to live in. My friend is ashamed of how we live together now."

"How much better?" said the flounder.

"How much better what?"

"How much better would you like your house to be?"

"I don't know," the fisherman said. "I didn't think to ask. Maybe my friend would like another room, to put guests in. And a window in the kitchen over the sink, and wood floors. And a bigger bed."

"Oil-modified urethane finish," asked the flounder, "or water-based polyurethane finish?"

"What?"

"For the floor," the flounder said.

"Oh," the fisherman said. "Well, I guess the oil-based finish would be better, because sometimes I track in water, when I come home from the sea and bring my catch in with me."

"It is done," said the flounder. "Go home."

"I can't go home yet," the fisherman said. "I haven't caught anything yet." But the flounder was already gone, so the fisherman stayed and fished a while longer, and then he went home. When he got there, there was a neat little garden out in front of the house full of red chickens scratching for grubs among the cabbages, and he opened the front door to find a sitting room with two fat armchairs in it. There was a window over the sink in the kitchen, and new copper pots hanging just above the stove. There was a new wireless in the dining room (they now had a dining room), and two very big beds in the master bedroom. His friend was in one of them. The wood floors had an oil-modified urethane finish.

"Oh," the fisherman said. "This is a much better house."

His friend said, "Then why do you look so cross?"

"I'm sorry," the fisherman said. "I don't mean to look cross. I like it very much, and I hope you will not be ashamed to have our friends visit any longer."

"Perhaps you do not look cross," his friend said. "Perhaps you are just sick. You do look sick."

"Perhaps I am sick," the fisherman said. "It has been a long day, and I have been out in the sun for longer than I should."

His friend said, "Why don't you get into my bed and rest? I don't mind if you use it."

"How lucky I am to have you for a friend," the fisherman said. His friend climbed out of bed, and the fisherman climbed in, and his friend went to the kitchen and brought him back a cup of hot tea.

The fisherman said, "Thank you, but I don't want any tea," and his friend sighed a long, low sigh.

"This is why people don't like helping you. Do you want people to like helping you?"

And the fisherman, who forgot he had not asked for his friend to help him, said, "Of course I do."

"Then drink your tea, please," his friend said. "Why do you make me regret doing nice things for you?"

That night the fisherman did not sleep very well at all. He had burned his tongue, and his new bed was too big.

"Do you think you will be happy to live here?" he asked his friend in the morning. "And not ashamed? I think we can live here very well," he added.

"We will think about it," his friend said. They had a quiet breakfast together.

The next day, after he had come home from the sea, the fisherman's friend said to him, "Our new house is lovely— too lovely for the kind of friends you have insisted on bringing around in the past. Go see the flounder tomorrow, and tell him that we need a better class of people to associate with us, to go with the house."

"What kind of people?" the fisherman asked.

"People of consequence," his friend said. "Interesting people. Attractive people. People I would not be ashamed to have here."

And the fisherman, who did not know his friend had been ashamed, did just that.

* * *

"Well, you're back again awfully soon," the flounder said.

"I did not know enough to be ashamed before I met you, flounder," said the fisherman. "But my friend, who is very helpful and who I am very lucky to have, is teaching me."

"What does your friend want, then?" the flounder asked.

"The people we associated with in our old house are no

longer fit for us," the fisherman said. "We would like a new class of people to be our friends."

The flounder said, "It's done," and disappeared. The fisherman sat in his boat for a long time. He forgot to put his hook in the water.

When he got home that night, his friend said, "Now you really do look sick. You should get into bed; a party would wear you out entirely."

"Are we having a party?" the fisherman said.

"I'm having some people over later," said his friend. "We'll be quiet, and I'll make sure no one disturbs you."

"Are you sure you don't want me to greet them?" the fisherman said. "I could rest first."

"Why would you want me to host a party and look after you at the same time?" his friend asked. "Could you please try just a little to make things easier for me, and get into bed, and rest?"

So the fisherman did. He said, "Talk to me, while I am resting?" What he was trying to say, of course, was, *I am sorry; please don't stop helping me.*

"All right," his friend said. "Let me think of a story to tell you." He sat back and thought. He thought and he thought. "I cannot think of a story to tell you."

"It's not important," the fisherman said.

His friend shook his head. "Obviously it is. It was important enough for you to ask me to stop and think of one while I am trying to get ready for our party, and now I won't be able to concentrate until I tell you a story, because you are sick and I want you to get better. I am not going to be able to get any of the things done that I wanted to, because of this."

"I'm sorry," the fisherman said. "I didn't mean it."

"Please don't lie to me on top of everything else," his friend said.

"I'm sorry," the fisherman said again. "I didn't mean it."

"Tomorrow you should go and ask the flounder for another house," said his friend, "because I do not think you like me to live with you. Then you could have all the peace and quiet you needed, and I would not bother you so much, if I had someone over."

"No," the fisherman said. "No, I do not want my own house; please do not ask me to do that, *please* don't."

"It's not for my own pleasure that I said it," his friend said. "I am only thinking of you."

"I am so sorry," the fisherman said, "only please do not ask me to leave you."

"I am going out to the front porch," his friend said, "and there I will walk up and down until I have thought of a story for you, even though it is very cold outside, and I have no coat. I will do this for you."

"Please don't," the fisherman said.

"Why are you making me feel guilty for trying to do something nice for you?" his friend said.

"I do not know how to stop hurting you," the fisherman cried. "I must be doing something very wrong." His friend went out to walk up and down the front porch, and the fisherman stole out of bed and left the house by the back entrance. He walked down to his little boat in the dark and pushed out to sea.

"Flounder," he called when he had sailed out a ways. "Flounder." The water was black and boiling. "Flounder."

The flounder appeared. "Fisherman," it said, "this was not exactly what I intended, when I told you I could give you something no one else could."

"What did you mean, then?" the fisherman said, and if he was crying, he could not help it.

"I could help you," the flounder said, "if you would ask me for something else, and not what you came out here to ask me."

"My friend wants me to wish for my own house," the fisherman said, "which makes me miserable, because I want to live with no one but my friend."

"You do not live with a friend," the flounder said. "I have seen your home and the one who lives there with you, he is no friend to you."

The fisherman snatched the flounder out of the sea with his right hand. It flashed and flopped all over the bottom of the boat. Next he tore out its gills with his thumbs and ran his fingers through its belly, from throat to tail, until its insides were quite clean. He threw the flounder's guts back into the sea, and then he went home. The party was over, and all of the guests had left. His friend was still walking up and down the porch, shivering and stamping. "Where have you been?"

"I have been to see the flounder for you," the fisherman

said. "It died." Then he went inside the house and took a shower.

After he went to bed, he heard a loud banging sound through the wall, and he got up.

"Why are you banging your head against the wall?" asked the fisherman.

"I hope that if I bang my head against the wall hard enough, it will help me to think of a story for you, because you are sick and I want you to feel better," said his friend.

"I am feeling much better now," said the fisherman. "I do not think I need a story anymore. I do not need anything now, I promise."

"Then get out of your bed and let me get into it," said his friend, "because now I feel terrible. Helping you has made me sick."

So the fisherman got out of his bed and his friend got in. The fisherman leaned against the wall for a minute, and his friend said, "*Please* get me a cup of tea. I got one for you. I shouldn't have to ask."

The fisherman said, "I'm sorry," and he went to the kitchen and fixed his friend a cup of tea.

His friend said, "You never want to help me. Why is it that you want to live with me, when I know you hate me?"

The fisherman said, "I don't hate you."

His friend said, "Don't sulk. You're so unpleasant when you sulk. Everybody says so."

The fisherman said, "Would you like me to tell you a story?"

"Yes," said his friend, "*if* you know one."

"Once upon a time," said the fisherman, "there were two good friends, one of whom was a fisherman. Two very good friends." He swayed a little, and then fell into a little heap on the hardwood floor.

"*Please*," his friend said from the bed, "stop being so dramatic. My tea has gotten cold."

"I don't think I'm very much better after all," the fisherman said.

His friend sighed. "Is it really that hard for you to care for me just a little, just once, when I've worn myself out caring for you? If it is, tell me and I'll go."

"I'm sorry," said the fisherman.

"You are always sorry," his friend said.

The fisherman got up and walked back to the kitchen, and accidentally banged his head against the doorway. "And don't just heat up the old tea," his friend said after him. "Bring me a fresh cup. My head aches from beating it against the wall for you."

"How's this, my darling?" the fisherman asked, carrying the steaming cup back into the room cupped between his hands.

But his friend did not answer.

His friend had fallen asleep.

Sources and Influences

1. The Daughter Cells
   - *"The Little Mermaid," Hans Christian Andersen*

2. The Thankless Child
   - *"Cinderella," Jacob and Wilhelm Grimm*
   - King Lear, *William Shakespeare*
   - The Ladder of Divine Ascent, *St. John Climacus*
   - *Lorica of St. Patrick, Irish-Christian prayer*
   - *The Divine Praises, Catholic prayer*
   - *Psalm 139*

3. Fear Not: An Incident Log
   - *The Book of Genesis*

4. The Six Boy-Coffins
   - *"The Six Swans," Jacob and Wilhelm Grimm*
   - *"The Twelve Brothers," Jacob and Wilhelm Grimm*

5. The Rabbit
   - The Velveteen Rabbit, *Margery Williams*

6. The Merry Spinster
   - Beauty and the Beast, *Jeanne-Marie Leprince de Beaumont*

7. The Wedding Party
   - *"The Goose-Girl," Jacob and Wilhelm Grimm*
   - *"The Earl of Mar's Daughter," Child ballad*
   - *"The Daemon Lover," Scottish ballad*

8. Some of Us Had Been Threatening Our Friend Mr. Toad
   - The Wind in the Willows, *Kenneth Grahame*
   - *"Some of Us Had Been Threatening Our Friend Colby,"*
     Donald Barthelme

9. Cast Your Bread Upon the Waters
   - *"Johnny Croy and His Mermaid Bride," Orkney folktale*
   - Summa Theologica, *Thomas Aquinas*

10. The Frog's Princess
    - *"The Frog Prince," Jacob and Wilhelm Grimm*

11. Good Fences Make Good Neighbors
    - *"The Fisherman and His Wife," Jacob and Wilhelm*
      Grimm
    - Frog and Toad Are Friends, *Arnold Lobel*

Acknowledgments

I want to thank Jos Lavery and Christian Brown for answering an unending barrage of text messages asking for their opinions on every change, no matter how minor, I made to this manuscript, like two extremely tolerant optometry patients—"Is this one better? Or is *this* one better?" There are no two people whose literary judgment I prize more, and this book has been immeasurably improved thanks to their thoughtful criticism.

Thanks are also due to my editor, Libby Burton, whose careful attention to detail at every stage of the publishing process has been a great relief and a help to me. I am especially grateful to my longtime agent, Kate McKean, who has only ever praised my successes, corrected my errors, and made me money. I wish everyone in the world were like her.

About the Author

MALLORY ORTBERG is the co-creator of *The Toast* and the author of the *New York Times* bestseller *Texts from Jane Eyre*.